Kiren Rai

Born and brought up in Uganda, East Africa, Kiren migrated to India in her early teens. She has been a newspaper reporter, college lecturer, media relations specialist and an e-content writer. She has written *The Sacred Indian Tarot,* a beautiful hand-drawn deck of tarot cards with 22 Major Arcana cards, combining the traditional elements of the tarot with a rich tapestry of Indian mythology and culture.

Kiren promotes upcoming and contemporary art, bringing together different mediums, cultural hues and individual styles from across the globe. *(http://arteindia.com/)*

Madhvi Ahuja

Madhvi comes from a business management and stock-broking background. A lifelong passion for writing, two creative writing courses, at the University of Oxford and at NYU, translated into a dream entrepreneurial venture—her very own start-up firm, 'The Writer's Web.' She provides content writing solutions for corporates and other professionals. *(www.thewritersweb.in)*

Madhvi is into fitness and is a trained Muay Thai fighter. She brings the same energy and fervour into her work. She also has an immense love for dogs, especially her golden lab, Maximus.

Cupidity—Ping Me, Love is the first novel she has co-authored.

Cupidity

Ping Me, Love

Kiren Rai & Madhvi Ahuja

Om Books International

First published in 2016 by

Om Books International

Corporate & Editorial Office
A-12, Sector 64, Noida 201 301
Uttar Pradesh, India
Phone: +91 120 477 4100
Email: editorial@ombooks.com
Website: www.ombooksinternational.com

Sales Office
107, Ansari Road, Darya Ganj,
New Delhi 110 002, India
Phone: +91 11 4000 9000
Fax: +91 11 2327 8091
Email: sales@ombooks.com
Website: www.ombooks.com

ISBN: 978-93-84625-42-9

Printed in India

10 9 8 7 6 5 4 3 2 1

We dedicate this book to each other, if we bring our near and dear ones into this, the dedication will run longer than the accepted word count!

In all seriousness, this book is dedicated to you, dear reader.

We hope you enjoy our piece of fiction and make it a part of your journey.

Contents

1

Salt & Pepper Shakers

The day began on a wrong note. The driver called in with an excuse and said he would be unable to come to work.

"Darn man! Just when I needed him the most," grumbled Tara as she put down her cell phone.

The driver, predictably, never showed up on those days when she was running late for work. Today was a busy one; she had a clincher of a meeting with an upcoming hotel and was already running behind schedule.

A successful interior designer, Tara loved her life and remained fairly occupied. Design was an obsession with her and she made a living out of it. Tara had studied Design and Architecture from one of the top schools in the US, the Rhode Island School of Design. She had an almost intuitive sense of style when it came to her clients and was recognised as one of the best layout architects in the city. Tara's style was quirky yet classy and she had built quite a reputation. She worked as a consultant with a few big architectural firms to cope with the large project load due to the retail boom.

Tara had joined a top architectural firm in New Delhi soon after her graduation, where she had met her husband Ranvir, a brilliant architect himself. Within months of seeing each other, in and out of work, Ranvir had proposed to her, and before she could say 'Jack Robinson', she was married to him. For Ranvir, it was love at first sight; he knew that she would be his wife. Sixteen years had gone by in a blink and today was just another day.

Tara rushed through the inner roads, over flyovers, and made the car screech to a halt in front of her son's school, in 15 minutes flat. She dropped off Neil—her 15-year-old son—for soccer practice and dashed home to get ready.

No longer was traffic rush restricted to office hours or specific mad days; nowadays, every day seemed like the special mad day. Fifteen years ago, when Tara first learnt to drive her beaten down second-hand Maruti 800—a hand-me-down from her husband—the roads were narrower, traffic was manageable and people were patient and polite. Things had changed drastically, the roads had become broader, layers of flyovers had popped up and people were far from being patient. Delhi's roads were like a jungle now and only the fittest survived. Tara began to put her things together—a list of 'to-take things' that she kept ticking off in her head—laptop, diary, portfolio, keys and a banana.

Breakfast in the car! Lovely! Run, run, run Tara!

She shimmied into a pair of her favourite skin-tight blue jeans with a classic white linen work shirt. She covered up with a black coat and a pair of black boots. A boho bag slung over her arm, she completed her rather chic look with her favourite pair of massive designer sunglasses. Tara always chose the classic simple look. She was elegant and chic in the same breath and comfortable in her own skin. She wouldn't have it any other way, trends came and went but she had her own identity to brandish. Be it in a professional space or as an individual, Tara wore an air of confidence around her, which people often percieved as arrogance. But she was far from it; Tara was straightforward, spoke her mind and didn't have a single manipulative bone in her body.

'Phew! Just about made it.'

Just when she was about to leave she remembered that she had to mail a prospective buyer regarding a residential project. Tara had worked late night on the project cost and details and wanted to send them to the client before noon.

She opened her mailbox, when a message popped up in a chat window at the bottom right corner of the screen.

> **(10:11 am) Pepper & Salt:** Girl at 42... Hmm... So when does this girl become a woman? I like the spirit... Up for a chat?

She sent her mail. *What was that?* Tara wondered as she hurried out of the house.

It all came back to her while she was driving. *Oh! The online dating site!* Her school friend Nalini had initiated her into it. Tara had all but forgotten her little adventure with her. *Ah! Now it made sense.*

> It was an innocuous March evening, Nalini had come over to spend the night. She was one of Tara's closest friends. They had spent their childhood together at a private boarding school in the hills. They trusted each other implicitly. Nalini had an early morning train to Jaipur and getting to the New Delhi railway station from Tara's place was an easier option. Tara and Nalini shared similar life paths, they were both creative people and held ethics as the cornerstone of their profession. They had strong opinions and

'moral' views that translated to success in their respective careers. Nalini was a film-maker and had various path-breaking documentaries to her credit. Her latest one had been for the ASI (Archaeological Survey of India), on the fusion of Hindu and Islamic architecture as evident on the Khirki Mosque. It had won her critical acclaim. Nalini was going through a rough phase in her life at that time. There was tremendous work pressure from an arrogant media partner; she had had a break-up, and her mother was constantly sick.

But when Nalini walked in, she was unrecognisable—glowing skin, laughter like a school girl, and she had shed over a stone. Her derrière was all taut and she flaunted her washboard abs! She had a lilt in her gait and was sporting a million-dollar haircut. Tara looked at her and gave a cocky smile, "Wow! What's with you, Nalsie?"

Nalini gave her a smug smile and said, "I'm happy, baby! I have a real nice guy in my life."

"Ah ha! No wonder, it all adds up," Tara's smile became mischievous. She added, "Trust us to still derive happiness from men! Ha ha ha... So where did you meet him?"

Why do we always want to validate our existence with a man's presence? It just doesn't feel complete. And Tara was okay owning that thought, sick of fighting it anyway.

"What a fortunate turn of events. Not just a man, but a nice man! This is like a cherry topping on a delicious hot fudge sundae."

Nalini relaxed and smiled, "He is a complete hot fudge sundae!"

After a couple of drinks and some merry conversation, Nalini brought her laptop out and logged into a dating site *www.cupidity.in*. They lounged on the two-seater by the window and enjoyed a perfect Delhi breeze.

Tara looked out of the window and commented, "This weather is reminding me of Charles Dickens."

Nalini completed her thought, "It was one of those March days when the sun shines hot and the wind blows cold: when it is summer in the light and winter in the shade."

"Wonderfully appropriate words. However, nothing will happen sitting by a windowsill. Those are bygone days, Tara. This," she pointed to her laptop, "is the latest; everyone finds people online now."

Pretty intrigued by the entire process, Tara leaned in and read over Nalini's shoulder. She showed Tara a few of the guys she was chatting with and out of the blue, Nalini said, "Hey Tara! Let's open an account for you! Ranvir is never in town, your life is dull enough; you probably have cobwebs down there. Let's add some pizzazz."

Tara's first reaction was reluctance, after all, she was a married woman, and it just didn't seem right. The thought of talking to some stranger online seemed desperate and frivolous. But Nalini persisted and showed her new beau Jai's profile.

Tara was quite impressed, "You found 'him' online? Not bad. What does he do?"

Nalini beamed, "He is the CEO of an MNC in Gurgaon. He is 48 and a widower, has two daughters who are studying in the US. He is brilliant at his work, without being cocky about it. And he has a gentle side to him that I like."

Nalini saw Tara relenting and before she could change her mind, Nalini opened an account for her, "Welcome to *Cupidity*! It is one of the most happening dating sites today. Okay, what handle do you want me to give you? Come on…it is only to add a little fun to your life! Relax."

After a moment's hesitation, Tara said, "What the heck! It is only in the virtual world; let's give it a shot… can't harm anybody. What's a…er… handle?"

"What name do you want to be called by?"

"Hmm!" She was totally intrigued and flummoxed. *A name for me? Can't figure one at random.* After a couple of potshots in the dark, it came to her.

"Hey Nalsie, how does 'Ubercool' sound?" she imagined herself having the ultimate benchmark when it came to being cool—attractive, chic and avant-garde.

"Ubercool?" Nalini checked Tara out. She was slim and fair with lustrous, black straight hair till her waist.

"I like it! It suits you."

"'Ubercool' it is!" Nalini quickly typed in that word in the Login name, and 'Ubercool' came alive.

Tara was befittingly the 'uber' woman in today's changing urban space. Eclectic and well read, she could hold her own. Tara was a perfect blend of a modern woman, juggling work and home efficiently.

Her thoughts went back to the message from a certain Pepper & Salt; she pondered over what kind of a guy he would be. Her curiosity in the online dating concept peaked. A firm sharp honk snapped her reverie. Her gaze fell on an impatient driver in the rear-view mirror. He was cussing her no end. Tara's focus shifted to the present and she concentrated on the forthcoming meeting.

As she walked into the property, she effortlessly slipped into her work mode. She mentally envisioned the Zen-like garden, the clean furniture, the bamboo floors and cool lights that were an interesting feature of the new property. The meeting went off well. All was on track and she would soon begin work.

Tara was glad to get back home after a busy day. She headed straight to her desktop as curiosity got the better of her. She logged onto *www.cupidity.in* as Ubercool and skimmed through Pepper & Salt's profile. Tara couldn't believe that she was actually using a dating site just to check the message from some random man, a complete stranger!

What's wrong with me?

Tara was the last person who needed validation on the Internet! And that too from someone unknown. However unnatural it seemed to her inherent nature, Tara just couldn't resist the urge to check this guy out.

Tara had never been short of male appreciation. She remembered the time when she had many suitors vying to take her out on a date. But all this was before Ranvir had come into her life. Tara was so consumed by her marriage, that the thought of any other man just didn't excite her. Things had changed. In their initial years together, it was all about 'them'. Now, it seemed like it was anything but them. Ranvir was a workaholic, always immersed in his work and travelled 20 days in a month. A random guy sending her a message made her feel like a 'woman'. She felt wanted. It had been a while since she had felt this way.

His profile read well to begin with. *I mean, he sounds cool.*

PROFILE

Name: Pepper & Salt

Brief description: I have a taste for the finer things in life and appreciate art in most forms. I love lengthy discussions about everything under the sun, and can hold a conversation on anything—from Sufism to politics, on the state of moral decline or the clash of civilisations. I don't smoke regularly, but love doing it, so let's just say I do. I choose the company I drink with, which is very limited, so let's just say I don't. I also like my coffee black!

He had left the rest of the questions on the profile format unanswered. *To the point.* He sounded well-heeled and seemed to share her interests in philosophy and history. *Wow, I thought it would be difficult to find men who can chat. This is a pleasant change. It would be fun to share some common turf.*

She did notice his personal life details as well—married, but in a complicated relationship. Also, the man had two kids. *Sounds perfect… Wouldn't make too many demands and pile on.*

Tara comtemplated messaging him back. *What's the harm anyway? Ranvir is out most of the time and it would do me good to have a buddy to chat with.*

For the last three years, Tara had got used to living on her own. Ranvir's assignments had been offshore mostly. This meant that she got to be with him only a couple of days every few months. She was used to juggling work, child and home pretty seamlessly now. Of late, Tara was beginning to get lonely; she could feel a chasm growing between Ranvir and herself. Also, Neil was entering into his rebellious teenage phase. The hormones were hitting him big time and more often than not, Tara was the punching bag. Sometimes, Tara got mad at Ranvir and thought, *He should come and take over Neil! After all, the young boy needs his father.*

Under all the complaints about the 'missing' father, she masked her own void—missing companionship of a partner, having a good time together, going for movies, walks and parties. Most of the parties they got invited to had couples and Tara had started feeling a bit awkward fielding 'unwarranted queries' from people. Questions like *Where is Ranvir? Poor you! Must be awful living on your own?* were beginning to irritate Tara.

She decided to go online and fill up the details on her profile with a little more thought before venturing into a conversation with anyone.

What the hell! A little male attention couldn't hurt anyone.

PROFILE

Name: Ubercool

Age: 45

City: New Delhi

Status: Married

Brief description: Fun, generous, gregarious, laptop addict, and a self-confessed 'chocoholic'...

What are you doing with your life: Finding myself

List a few of your favourite things

Books: I am a history buff, so my favourite authors are Indu Sundaresan, Alex Rutherford, Conn Iggulden, Ashok Banker, Amitav Ghosh. I also like Eckhart Tolle and Wayne Dyer.

Music: Bob Dylan, the reggae music of Bob Marley, Santana, Cliff Richard, Paul Anka... and... Actually all of the '70s and '80s. I also like Advaita, Shakira and Lady Gaga. I love all kinds of chants, be it Vedic, Mayan or Tibetan.

Food: Thai, Chinese, Italian and South Indian

What do you spend most of your time thinking about: The Paranormal! How to brew the perfect Sabbath's brew!

What is a typical Friday night for you: I am chilling like all other nights, but I am game for some fun.

The most private thing you are willing to admit: I am a rabid cleanliness freak and a lousy driver.

Who should contact you: Straight men, men above 40, interesting men, good-looking men, men confident in their own skin.

People should message if: You are interested in good conversation. Being bright and exploratory are prerequisites. I just want a friend to while away some time. Nothing serious and no mush please!

Okay, that wasn't so bad.

Neil walked in just as Tara wrapped up entering her profile information. She always felt a surge of pride when she set eyes on her son. Tall, athletic and spritely, Neil was a take on his father. Tara thought to herself, *Yes, I really did a good job with this one.* He was funny, articulate and someone who cared about other people. Neil was helpful, interesting to be around with and was very charismatic. *Yes...He is my good guy.*

Okay, she couldn't take full credit for it, but she had put in real effort in his growing years to teach him things that would help him get by in this big world. Now she felt that

Ranvir needed to take over with some of the more important transitions in their son's life. Neil felt he knew everything and that mom was plain dumb.

"Hi Neil! How was your day?"

"Okay. Nothing great. The usual."

"How was soccer practice?"

"Good. Match coming up," Neil answered dryly. He had come back from his Math and Science tuitions and was famished. He quickly grabbed an apple from the fruit bowl and took a bite.

"At least wash the apple, if not your hands! Anyway, it's almost dinner time."

"Aww mom!"

"Don't 'aww-mom' me, Neil. How's your science project coming along? Have you revised for your tests?"

"Mom! Chill! Everything is in control. Can I take a breather? I have just come back from my classes…just so you know!"

Tara ignored the barb and said, "If everything's in control, young man, how is it that your grades are steadily plummeting every term?"

"*Uff*… Not now, mom," as Neil stood up to go to his room.

"You don't read your textbooks, you don't revise, you are lagging in your project work… How is everything in control? Life is not only soccer and games, Neil."

As Neil walked away towards his room, Tara realised her futile attempt to engage her son for a meaningful chat.

"Clean your room… It looks as if it has just survived a tornado. And please…"

"No mom," Neil said loudly, his temper rising. He had his own ways to retaliate, "I will not clean my room, I will not read a book and I think I can relax by seeing a movie. C'mon mom, stop nagging!"

Both father and son were grating on Tara's nerves. "No Neil! You have your finals just round the corner. You have been so busy with your soccer matches that you are running behind in all your projects. Why can't you work your butt off and target getting good grades and finish all your pending work? What's wrong with you?" Tara said, a little exasperated.

Neil did not bother replying. Tara could hear the thud of his room door banging behind him.

Of late, Tara was having a tough time setting rules as Neil was beginning to feel assertive and trying every trick in the game to break all boundaries. Neil's grades were on the decline, homework was taboo and project deadlines were a thing of the past. Tara tried to be patient with him but Neil was getting a bit out of hand. Every time she spoke to Ranvir about him, he would say, "Don't despair, it will be fine. Boys will be boys. Don't confront him Tara, just be flexible and don't patronise him. Negotiate, don't confront."

It was easy to say all that Ranvir spoke over the phone, but even his teachers were pointing out that Neil was a bit distracted in class. She had spoken to a counsellor at school and they subtly hinted that the father needed to come in and take things over.

Tara loved Neil to bits; she tried treating him like an adult and setting achievable goals. But, at times, she would just fly off the handle and lose further ground with him.

Darn, why can't Ranvir just come back? He had enormous patience and somehow could get through to Neil. She kept telling Ranvir to come back and take over as a parent, to make a 'man' out of his son. "He needs to be more responsible with his own life," Tara had said to Ranvir one day when she had called him. Admittedly, Tara had a bad temper and Neil looked at his mom as the 'Tiger Mom'.

Another point of dissent between the couple was that Ranvir's parenting style was diametrically opposite to hers. Instead of being an authoritative figure for their child, Ranvir tried to be a friend to Neil. Hence, the son bonded better with his dad. Neil chose to spend most of his time with his dad because he would rather be without the rules. She felt Neil was like the rope in a tug of war, torn between two directions. Tara felt like banging her head with all the dissonance at home.

If Ranvir is so confident that this is the way to bring up his child, why doesn't he get back here and take responsibility and accountability? It's easy to be sitting 1,000 miles away and being the good cop.

Often, Tara felt that Ranvir undermined her authority by giving in to Neil and this was a real sore point with her. For her, parenting was all about one picking up the slack from the other or filling in when one needed rest; but here it was a different story altogether. Tara's missing companionship with Ranvir was her 'perceived wrong' that she could still live by, but when it came to Neil, not having the father figure physically present and involved, was something Tara was not ready to accept.

She went back to the computer... *Kids!* For the time being, the dating site seemed more apt to spend her energy on, rather than battling a teenager.

Now that she had filled in her profile details, Tara decided to send Pepper & Salt a message:

> **(9:10 pm) Ubercool:** Hi! thank you for your message. Sorry for the delay. sure, let's chat… how u doing? tell me more abt urself

And then, almost immediately, a window popped open.

Aah! So this is what the chat window or the instant messenger thingy looks like. Pepper & Salt was online and he responded immediately to the message:

> **(9:11 pm) Pepper & Salt:** Hi. Thanks for replying to my message. I am lots of things… but to begin with, I'm 45, fit, kind of distinguished looking, wear formals most of the time, speak fluent English and try to walk with a swagger :)
>
> **(9:12 pm) Ubercool:** Ha ha ha! funny! I like your attitude. what do you do?
>
> **(9:12 pm) Pepper & Salt:** I work
>
> **(9:13 pm) Ubercool:** Yeah, I figured… but as in…
>
> **(9:13 pm) Pepper & Salt:** I am a management consultant. I basically fix others. It's a lot easier than fixing oneself.
>
> **(9:14 pm) Ubercool:** Ha!
>
> **(9:15 pm) Pepper & Salt:** So, ordinarily, I should wonder what a nice married lady might be doing on this site...but maybe, I don't really wonder. It's nice to chat with people, I understand :)
>
> **(9:16 pm) Ubercool:** Yup! I'm bored at the moment, so suits me to chat with a stranger

She quite liked the name Pepper & Salt and found something interesting about him. The chat went around the usual introductory banter of testing waters and sussing each other out. Tara liked this easy conversation, found him witty, and decided to continue messaging him:

(9:38 pm) Ubercool: ok, so tell me a bit more about yourself

(9:38 pm) Pepper & Salt: Now that you have checked out my profile?

(9:38 pm) Pepper & Salt: I can sense the stunned, how-did-he-know look on ur face… Such a newbee, haha! It comes up on the notifications… Don't worry, I ain't stalking you.

(9:38 pm) Ubercool: Hahahaha… ooh hahahaha

(9:39 pm) Pepper & Salt: I'm an endearing foible with all my idiotic idiosyncrasies et al.

"We shall not cease from exploration
And the end of all our exploring
Will be to arrive where we started
And know the place for the first time."

—T.S. Eliot, *Little Gidding V*

Great touch…it is like he knows how to score with me!

(9:39 pm) Ubercool: Interesting. So, married with two kids, what are you looking for here?

(9:39 pm) Pepper & Salt: Women… but not in a relationship sense

(9:40 pm) Ubercool: Me too, I'm just looking to fill some time on my hands

(9:40 pm) Pepper & Salt: Hmm… Your intentions seem very innocent, but can you deny the draw of the devil?

(9:40 pm) Ubercool: Umm! The draw of the devil is always very exciting; what u can't get is always alluring, isn't it?

(9:40 pm) Pepper & Salt: You know what is even more alluring? The little possibility of getting that which seems unattainable

And so, the light chat—that bordered on flirtatious banter—went on for a while. It became friendly and familiar, quicker than Tara had anticipated.

(10:02 pm) Ubercool: What kind of women do you like?

(10:05 pm) Pepper & Salt: How can one ever define... if I based it on past relationships, I will only come up with usual clichés

(10:06 pm) Ubercool: ok, So don't come up with the regular clichés. just describe whatever comes to mind

(10:07 pm) Pepper & Salt: attractive, intelligent, witty, warm, fun, funny

(10:07 pm) Pepper & Salt: passionate curious

(10:08 pm) Pepper & Salt: slim and athletic

(10:09 pm) Pepper & Salt: smile to die for

(10:09 pm) Pepper & Salt: well read

(10:10 pm) Ubercool: Now that's a tall order, what do you look like?

(10:10 pm) Pepper & Salt: They say that when there is mystique, or say, enigma, a man seems very attractive.

(10:15 pm) Ubercool: Va Va Vroom, Ha Ha! But for now, I'll have to say good night to you, we'll chat tomorrow.

It was nearing 10:30 pm and Tara was beginning to get sleepy. It had been a long and tiring day and she did not want to miss her daily good night ritual with Neil. She needed to hug and kiss her son good night if she was in town. *Don't know how long that will last, but I intend to tuck him in as long as I can help it!* She smiled at the thought, shut the doors and turned off the lights.

Tara smiled at the thought of her chat buddy while getting into bed. *He sounded so umm…yummy! Jeez, my definition of yummy has changed drastically.* It was about the conversation being intoxicating, far from what she would have had in her 20s. She visualised him as this tall, dignified looking man with 'Pepper & Salt' hair, someone who wrote well… *I am sure he has a great voice and that irresistible X factor,* she thought as she turned off her bedside lamp.

Her thought suddenly went to Ranvir who was on an assignment in Singapore. She looked at the watch. 'He must be asleep now, it's late for him.' When she had first met Ranvir, the thing that struck her about him was his good looks. Six feet tall, Ranvir was fair and had almond honey-coloured eyes. Ranvir was quite a looker. He was also highly educated, confident with an inimitable presence. Tara thought life got perfect when she started dating him. However, over time, their marriage began to get staid and boring. Ranvir was a workaholic. For him, self-actualisation meant work. With time, it became normal for her to accept that she had no place in Ranvir's world.

He had very little interest for much else, especially for a concept like marriage. As Tara dozed off, her last thoughts were, *I wish things had turned out differently… How I miss having a companion…a partner. We had that…I wish Ranvir hadn't drifted away on his own. When was the last time Ranvir told me he loved me? Or took me out for dinner? Our relationship has become so matter of fact. When was it that I lost touch with him? I don't want to be married just for the sake of it. I can't think of anything lonelier than spending the rest of my life with someone I can't talk to…*

Tara woke up the next morning with a strange feeling of unease, after a restless night of tossing and turning. She couldn't exactly put her finger on what, but just a brooding sense of disquiet, like a knot in the bottom of her gut. Tara rose and walked slowly towards the balcony. The day reflected her mood—cloudy and gloomy. *Why was it that if never called, Ranvir never bothered to call either?* Days could go by and it never occurred to him to call and check on his family. *On me.* It wasn't as though Ranvir was a bad husband; he was just not an involved husband.

Tara loved her morning coffee. She liked to brew her own cup of java every morning; it was her ritual to get the day started. She was just about walking into the kitchen to switch on the electric kettle when the doorbell rang. Naina walked into her flat.

"Morning."

Naina was a long-time friend who lived in the same neighbourhood as Tara. They met some 15 years ago in the elevator of the apartment building. They both hit it off like a house on fire and became good buddies. They would often visit each other and hang out, go for movies, take the kids out, go shopping, and do the usual fun stuff together.

Hot, smoky and dusky, Naina had just turned 36, but looked much younger. Totally into fitness, she had the figure of a 16-year-old and a face of a 27-year-old. Her smouldering hot eyes and berry red lips made her absolutely irresistible and she had a fan following among men who were eager to hook up with her. Recently divorced, Naina too was continually in a flap trying to juggle a job, kids, and a hectic social life.

Much had changed in the recent past. When Naina was married, she ran a successful export business with her husband. When things went sour between them, Naina was forced to leave the business and fend for herself. With enough only for child support, she took up a job.

Post her divorce, she had moved into an apartment in Tara's housing complex, and had sent her kids off to a boarding school. She was in a tricky phase of her life and Tara was aware of it. She had seen Naina through some dark times.

"Hi, perfect timing. I am certainly glad to see you."

"Why thank you, and I, you!" Naina said in a mock formal tone.

Tara laughed, "Silly, was going through a bit of a low. The usual, Ranvir and his absence from my life." Tara said as she hugged Naina.

Naina hugged her back, "I'm here. Let's have coffee first."

This was a familiar routine—Naina often dropped by on her way back from the gym. Tara poured the coffee and they both stepped out onto the balcony. Tara lived in a high rise building with a fabulous view of the cityscape. The balcony was her own little retreat from the hustle and bustle of everyday life and her favourite spot in the flat.

Naina too looked a bit low this morning. Tara decided to drop her own tales of woe and probe further. It turned out that Naina had had a fight with Rahul, her current boyfriend, who was also her boss. This wasn't out of the ordinary knowing that Naina was insecure about Rahul. This time it was over his flirting openly with Prerna, the frequent flier at the club.

Tara always wondered why Naina put up with Rahul and his arrogance and didn't have the confidence to start out afresh. Tara suspected that after her divorce, Naina took to Rahul as her lifeline. She was playing it safe. Tara was convinced that Naina needed to meet more people and keep her options open. She often ticked Naina, "Don't put all your eggs in one basket. You are stupid, you should explore!"

"What is with you? You look like you had a rough night too," Naina said, as she took a sip of her coffee.

"You know how it is...Ranvir. It's too lonely, all by myself. But...forget all that, I have the perfect solution for your stupid Rahul woes! I had a good time last evening..."

She told Naina about *www.cupidity.in* and threatened to create Naina's profile when they met next.

"Have you lost it!" Naina laughed. She knew that Tara didn't care much for Rahul because of his lack of commitment.

"Whatever...you will thank me. One of these days, I am going to do this for you."

Later that afternoon, Tara stretched while seated on her office chair, and decided to take a break. She logged onto *www.cupidity.in*. Tara had to admit that despite herself, she was beginning to enjoy the online experience of dating. She had over 20 visitors, loads of messages and a multitude of hits. "Wowee!" she said aloud. Life never got so busy for her. *Whoa! I'm in demand. I mean look at me...I'm quite the belle of the netizens club.*

She went through a few more messages casually, a few visitors' profiles and felt a wave of disappointment. Most of the messages were from young boys, older men, men with bad diction and the flakers—desperate men hitting on her. *These guys are such airheads; I wouldn't give them even a second of my time.* She was just about to shut her laptop when she saw a new message from Pepper & Salt in her chat window.

Over the next few days, she ignored everyone else on the website. She quite enjoyed chatting with Pepper & Salt. Tara felt, in her very core, that Pepper was the perfect man, the kind of man she had been looking for…all her life. *Well, that's a bit of an exaggeration, more like the man that I am searching for presently!*

His unassailable manner made her melt inside. She imagined Pepper & Salt to be a self-confident man who could light up the room with his charisma. Pepper & Salt seemed to know exactly what he wanted and had a story about how he always got what he desired. He would so often say, "Grab the moment and make life happen." She liked the easy repartee, the witty interjections and his command on the language. The fact that Pepper & Salt could talk well, coupled with his sense of humour, were the reasons that Tara allowed him into her world. Tara was a real stickler for essential standards of articulation and education as a whole. Pepper & Salt stood out in the crowd and Tara related to him on an intellectual level. But she was a bit shocked when her chat with Pepper & Salt took on a very personal tone.

(04:04 pm) Pepper & Salt: I just left you a message… and here you are! Hi…

(04:04 pm) Ubercool: Hi Pepper. Yes you did. I just logged on.

(04:04 pm) Pepper & Salt: So lady, picking up where we left off… is all ok with your marriage?

(04:04 pm) Pepper & Salt: the reason i ask is that…

(04:05 pm) Ubercool: kinda…

(04:05 pm) Pepper & Salt: I have seen more than one woman here, who is married but unhappy

(04:05 pm) Pepper & Salt: and is hence here

(04:05 pm) Ubercool: you know marriage is tough. sometimes I wonder why I didn't remain single. I would probably have enjoyed a sense of freedom. In a marriage, one's personal space is so tied down to a spouse and kids. u know what? I think sabbaticals should be made legal in marriages!

(04:08 pm) Pepper & Salt: Haha... I really don't want to intrude

(04:08 pm) Pepper & Salt: but what's really wrong with your marriage?

(04:09 pm) Ubercool: Hubby is a workaholic, he's been on offshore consultancies for the last 3 years

(04:09 am) Ubercool: he is busy "finding" himself while I take care of home and hearth

(04:09 pm) Pepper & Salt: ah ha!

(04:09 pm) Ubercool: have had enough of it now... am angry like hell

(04:10 pm) Pepper & Salt: funny how you throw in Maslow and self-actualisation

Tara had to finish some office work and excused herself from the chat. The conversation then resumed at night, post dinner.

(10:10 pm) Ubercool: Maslow???????

(10:10 pm) Pepper & Salt: some idiot

(10:10 pm) Pepper & Salt: favourite with corporate assholes

(10:10 pm) Pepper & Salt: talks about the hierarchy of needs—from basic ones to self-actualisation

(10:11 pm) Ubercool: Ya... to leave a good-looking, intelligent, warm wife behind...

(10:11 pm) Pepper & Salt: Modest?

(11:06 pm) Ubercool: so if you have a modicum of happiness just keep it

(11:07 pm) Pepper & Salt: not really

(11:07 pm) Pepper & Salt: why can't you make it happier?

(11:07 pm) Ubercool: I have a stay-away husband

(11:08 pm) Ubercool: I am trying real hard and i hope to get him back

(11:11 pm) Pepper & Salt: ha ha

(11:11 pm) Pepper & Salt: find a romantic artist

(11:11 pm) Pepper & Salt: and have a fling

(11:13 pm) Ubercool: No! that could be dangerous... I don't want any emotional yo-yoing

(11:13 pm) Pepper & Salt: you are cared of falling in love?

(11:13 pm) Pepper & Salt: scared*

(11:14 pm) Ubercool: yup. true

(11:14 pm) Pepper & Salt: Have an impersonal affair with an artist then!

(11:15 pm) Ubercool: what is impersonal about an affair?

(11:16 pm) Pepper & Salt: believe me

(11:16 pm) Pepper & Salt: i have seen quite a few who think it can be impersonal

(11:16 pm) Ubercool: ya, I suspect you could do that, but not me

(11:18 pm) Pepper & Salt: i could... Yes I am looking for exactly that and nothing more.

The conversations with Pepper & Salt would go on and off and continue whenever they found time. They seemed to be making time for each other. Tara was surprised at the effort she made to connect with Pepper & Salt online. She looked forward to the evenings when she would exchange notes on the day gone by in an easy-going banter with Pepper & Salt. Tara was beginning to enjoy engaging in conversation and would find any excuse to open her laptop. Gradually, she found herself thinking about Pepper & Salt's chats all through the day and snippets of their chats would bring a smile to her face.

Tara wanted to know what Pepper was expecting from her. At this stage she was beginning to get confused about what she needed. On one hand, she was very clear that she was not looking for an illicit affair; the dishonesty of it was completely off-putting. But on the other hand, she couldn't deny the fact that she was having fun with Pepper & Salt. She shared an amazing mental chemistry with him and in her mind's eye, she imagined him as the perfect 'Prince Charming'—suave, good-looking, intellectual guy with a stately bearing. She dug a little deeper one day.

(03:40 pm) Ubercool: Pepper, what brings you to this specific chat-site?

(03:42 pm) Pepper & Salt: I could easily cook up a story, but I want to be honest with you. You are so straightforward. I think I should be too.

(03:42 pm) Ubercool: Life is too short to not be straightforward.

(03:42 pm) Pepper & Salt: My wife was diagnosed with breast cancer 9 yrs ago. We fought it together and she is fine now. But...

(03:42 pm) Ubercool: Oh!

(03:43 pm) Pepper & Salt: Life became lonely. Somehow, over time, we have completely disconnected from each other. Don't misunderstand, I love her to bits, but... well, we have not been physical... we live in separate rooms.

Tara was speechless. She did not know what to say, she did not expect such candidness. *There are so many lonely people out there. In marriages. Stuck. Alone.*

Over the next few weeks, Tara was obsessively logging on to *www.cupidity.in*. It felt like her regular routine interfered with the 'meaningful' chats that she had with Pepper & Salt. This man was like a breath of fresh air to her otherwise monotonous existence.

He loved poetry and sent her random excerpts in her inbox. Tara was impressed with his love for literature and all the quotes from Rumi that he kept sending.

He told her he was considering writing a book. She was made to read certain chapters of his book of short stories and was smitten by his style. She liked the philosophical space she shared with him. It was a contrast to her husband calling such conversation 'intellectual masturbation'!

One random afternoon...

(03:34 pm) Pepper & Salt: Here is Rumi for you, don't take it seriously though. It is the only one I can remember right now: "Live where you fear to live. Destroy your reputation, be notorious."

(03:35 pm) Ubercool: Hey, you are supposed to be a good influence on me. I am pretty mad any way and don't need too much prompting. Love today's Rumi fix. Though suspect it is yours in the making...

(03:40 pm) Pepper & Salt: So, now what? We are married... Would a meeting seem tricky? Perhaps I will have to share more than usual through messaging

(03:41 pm) Ubercool: I still can't put a finger on you. Would be nice if you could send a picture as well

(03:41 pm) Pepper & Salt: What's a picture when two minds meet?

(03:42 pm) Ubercool: *Touché.* For that thought, you can buy me coffee one of these days. Our minds can meet in person.

It was early May, almost two months since they had first met online; Pepper asked her out for coffee a few times. Tara kept fobbing it off saying she was busy or pressed for time.

She didn't really want to meet him, although, she had to admit that there was great chemistry between them. Almost every topic took on a romantic and mildly sexual undertone. Although they never talked sex, the enticing nature of the innuendoes opened the floodgates of wanton thoughts.

Strangely, one day out of the blue, it happened. It was about 11 am and Tara was taking it easy, in bed. She had decided to bunk work and lounge in her jammies. She was curled up with a book that had been ignored far too long. Her phone beeped. It was her *www.cupidity.in* phone app. It had been a month since she had downloaded it on her smartphone. How else was she to keep in touch with Pepper & Salt on a regular basis?

Pepper & Salt: Hey, so where did you say you live?

Ubercool: Panchsheel

Pepper & Salt: Oh great! i'm coming to that part of the town, close to that area! But that is not why I asked... And well, maybe this is fate.

Ubercool: What?

Pepper & Salt: Want to meet? I could see you in half an hour.

Tara sat up. This just got real. She didn't respond in confusion. *I really didn't intend to meet anyone from this site. What now?*

Pepper & Salt: I am not joking, sweetheart. I want to meet you today

Pepper & Salt: Are you there? Did you fall off your chair? Ha ha!

Finally, Tara replied after a couple of minutes, but it seemed like an eternal wait for Pepper & Salt.

Ubercool: So, if we meet, how will I recognise you?

Pepper & Salt: Well, it isn't that difficult... I would say I'm a bit overweight, but just about. And of course, I am blessed with a great mop of hair, my barber often tells me that my hair is the envy of most women. Ha ha!

Ubercool: Whoa... Now that is a load of an answer

Ubercool: Ok, let's do this. See you at 12.

Tara was a little curious, imagining the dapper description that she had of him. For a guy who wrote well, she assumed that he was not only appealing to the mind, but would also be physically attractive. The fantasy extended to certain sophistication with a baritone voice, tall, and a well-propotioned physique. Dapper and dashing were the words that popped in Tara's head.

They planned to meet at a café near her place. She waited for a guy from *Mad Men*—classic good looks, distinguished mindset with a commanding presence. *He talks well and is a step ahead in philosophy and literature; he is the complete package.*

She entered the café and there was nobody inside. *What's keeping him? Is this some online joke?* Suddenly, she got a message: 'Stuck in traffic. See you in 10.'

Tara was way too nervous about this. *This is too random and so not something I thought I would do!* She decided to order a fresh lime soda. The emotional excitement of the date ran so high that she fidgeted nervously while she waited. She adjusted her hair and looked at herself in the mirror for the 100th time.

She was pleased at her reflection and took pride in her flawless complexion, long hair, slim waist and long legs. Always a head turner, she was used to the appreciative glances men gave her and was confident she would make quite an impact on Pepper & Salt.

Suddenly, she felt his presence and looked up to see a man walking towards her table with a beckoning smile. *Could this be him?*

All of five-feet-four inches, the man in front was fat, swarthy, dark, with pockmarks on his face. He barely reached her shoulder. The sweep of his hair, like a Mohawk, grew from one ear to the other, apparently covering a bald patch. His hair was clearly all 'salt' and nowhere near the 'pepper' that he claimed in his name. 'Nothing', absolutely nothing, about his look was close to anything he claimed. *Or as I imagined!*

Tara was so overwhelmed by his appearance that she almost gasped out aloud. *What happened to the distinguished gentleman—tall and charming?* Meeting Pepper & Salt sent a palpable shock through her entire being; she almost lost control of her facial muscles as her jaw fell open. *Could this be the man I had been losing sleep over?*

She couldn't believe that this was the same man she had been chatting with for so long. She felt a wave of repulsion run through. *Gosh! He looks…unfortunate!* That was the most polite adjective that popped in her head. *Oh crap! What have I gotten myself into?*

He walked towards her table, offered his hand and said with a smile, "Hi! I'm Gaurav. What a pleasure to meet you, Ubercool."

Pleasure my foot! Tara was so startled, she felt deceived. She got up, collected her things, left a 100 rupee note for the drink, and with a curtness she didn't know she possessed, blurted out, "I need to leave!" and left the café without an explanation.

She hurried out of the café. Her first reaction was to get as far as she could from the scene. The whole situation was so hilarious that she burst into laughter, much to the surprise of the passers-by. She reached the car, pulled out of the parking and called Ranvir in the middle of his working day. She got his voicemail. She was going to hang up, but left him a message instead.

"Hey, what you doing? I just wanted to tell you that I love you, why don't you just come back? Take a few days off, I miss you."

She opened the *Cupidity* app on her mobile and hit the 'Block User' tab on Pepper & Salt's profile. She then felt better, the whole meeting with Pepper & Salt had left her feeling a bit rattled. *What on earth about Pepper & Salt was distinguished? He looked like a 60-year-old Lothario, old enough to be a grandfather!*

She was a bit surprised that she could have been so gullible. He seemed so great, so perfect, so smooth, so enigmatic… *But what lies! What a downer. Be gone!* The special guy did not turn out to be so special after all. Enough of this rubbish, no more chatting, and she decided to take a break from the dating website. *I was so stupid to think that it was so easy.*

2

Hanging On

Tara spent the rest of the day feeling rather ashamed of her reckless behaviour, promising to herself that she would be more careful the next time.

Pepper & Salt was quite a character. Tara had to hand it to him, he had her completely drawn. That man had built a larger-than-life persona and his foibles had gotten her hooked. She couldn't help wondering, *how was his online presence so mismatched with his real personality?* She couldn't get over her escapade with Pepper. He probably would have been shy and an introvert playing out a role in the virtual world; a typical case of the recluse with an alter ego. *Hmm! Goes on to show that under the cloak of anonymity one can take on any garb. In a way, it frees one from social niceties and helps loosen up.*

She felt awkward talking to strangers. She was never a great one for small talk, but the anonymity of a chat room made it much easier to talk to people. Also, in a strange way, she felt chatting was not cheating. For her, this was a means of killing her loneliness. These virtual conversations removed any guilt that she would have had if she were to be spending time with a man in reality.

Tara walked over to Naina's place. Over wine, she narrated the entire Pepper & Salt fiasco to Naina. She had Naina in peals of laughter as she described the incident. She told how she began to appreciate Ranvir a lot more after that wreck of a meeting with her now-ex chat buddy. She wished things with Ranvir could change, but her evenings remained long. So, she decided to give *www.cupidity.in* one last shot.

"Are you serious?" Naina said, still laughing. "Come on, maybe we are too old for this stuff."

Tara did a mock shimmy, "Hey, we are *not* that old!"

Naina laughed even harder, "Stop…ha ha ha! Shut up woman! Ha ha ha!"

"Don't worry! I will take it easy on 'Cupidity'. I will engage in a conversation only after a photograph exchange. But engage, I will! Chatting online is interesting… There is no saying what a reaction to a potential date would be; probably, it is best to do a video chat."

Tara continued, "But you know, I have never seen a man in such a state. Why is it that most women need the company of men to feel complete? I keep oscillating between feeling fulfilled with my own life to having a complete sense of emptiness without Ranvir."

"Look at us two gorgeous women on a Friday night, dressed to kill, but no one to take the bait!" said Naina as she refilled her glass.

Tara expected a narration of some dramatic episode with Rahul. She rolled her eyes and asked, "What did that douche do now?"

Again, and for the millionth time, Rahul had ditched dinner plans with some cockamamie excuse. At the back of her mind, Naina knew Rahul was at some bar with some woman, and his repetitive story of 'charm' that she fell for long ago.

Naina worked at Rahul's relocation company. Although being a divorcee was tough, Naina tried her best to get her life back on track. A lot of men looked at her as an easy lay, and she was used to getting propositioned by so-called 'nice gentlemen'. Naina's stand-offish stance at most times deterred the unecessary overtures. She was often surprised at the so-called 'happily' married men who boldly came forward to 'support' in the guise of wanting to get into bed. When she started to date Rahul, her boss, thankfully, she did not have to face such a situation.

Despite a busy existence, Naina was an ardent fan of the gym—mind, body and all that jazz. She was always on the move.

She kicked off her pumps and tucked her feet beneath the cushions on the sofa as she turned towards Tara. She took a huge sip of her wine and whispered, "I am tired of being treated like a doormat by Rahul." She looked up, the hurt reflected in her eyes, "And you know what hurts even more? He knows the emotional bullshit I have been through with my divorce. He behaves like he doesn't care. I lean on him for support and he is just not there. Does he even give a damn?"

Tara listened, all the while turned to her laptop where the *www.cupidity.in* screen came alive. She had heard this story many times over. Tara looked up, "Okay, enough! I am sick of hearing how that man is treating you. What nauseates me further is that you put up with it instead of just dumping him! Look at this, there is a world of men out there—kind, funny, intelligent and sometimes all three clubbed into one man. Basically, all that's not Rahul!" She gave Naina a wicked smile.

Naina laughed. "You really don't like him, do you?" She smiled, the thought of someone being nice to her while she 'dumped' Rahul gave her cathartic relief.

"All eggs in one basket! You, missy, are in big trouble." While Naina wavered, Tara continued, "I am married, it holds me back. Rather, I hold myself back on that account. You are single. Take the risk, my dear! You totally can."

Tara persuaded Naina to create a profile on the website. She had been prodding her for many weeks to join the site. Finally, sick of the nagging, Naina gave in and took the plunge. "What the heck! It's not like there is very much happening in my life. Let's give it a shot, Tara."

The friends created 'Temptress 007' with a to-the-point profile:

PROFILE

Name: Temptress 007

Age: 36

City: New Delhi

A brief description: Tall, dark and vivacious. Single and recently divorced. Looking to get back on my feet, put on my dancing shoes and have a good time in life. Currently wearing my roller skates—juggling a job, hectic social life and kids... Yes! Boys, stay away! I am looking for a man. (Seriously... no one below 35 years please!)

What are you doing with your life: Working in an international relocation company. It's quite hectic!

List a few of your favourite things

I love socialising and networking. I am high on life with loads of energy!

Movies: English movies, all genres!

Music: All kinds of music. Love the '70s and the '80s!

Things you could never do without: My cell phone! My energy. My gym. Friends. Cigarettes.

What do you spend most of your time thinking about: The perfect life… and the delusion of it!

Who should contact you: Straight guys, between 35-45. Ideally, who live near me, are single and interested in long-term dating.

People should message you if: You have a sense of humour and are looking for an interesting conversation sans baggage!

Naina already felt smug with this profile. Tara insisted she be straightforward about everything. Profile done, they both called it a night. *Nights always seem to come out from nowhere and are like life creating a balance between the crappy and the beautiful. I, for the most part, do love my life,* Naina thought as she fell asleep.

Come Monday, Naina stepped into her regular routine as she logged on to her computer at work. Post midday, over coffee, she decided to take a break and check out *www.cupidity.in. What could've possibly happened in this much time?*

Naina logged in and… *Whoa!* There were 30 messages and 50 visitors all in one weekend. Well, she certainly did not expect this! It meant that nearly 80 per cent of the people who visited her profile actually wrote to her—Temptress 007! *You badass girl, you!* Naina suddenly felt a surge of excitement run through her. Just having come through a divorce, Naina always felt that maybe she wasn't good enough…in some irrational way, she felt a bit lesser or was made to feel like that in many situations. It was interesting how people accepted a woman in the stereotypical roles of a wife, a mother, and a daughter, whereas a single woman divorced and living on her own was always umm…'suspect'. This was exciting as Naina could be whoever she wanted. Her natural caution gave way to certain exuberance Naina hadn't felt in ages.

She started filtering her messages and the profiles of the people who had checked out her profile. She realised that the elimination process here was easy to execute. It was more like speed dating; the person on the other side got one sentence, or maybe two, before you decided his worth. *How judgemental! But how empowering!* Naina reckoned. *Life is too short to not have certain standards. Okay lady, let's see what you have on your plate today.*

Already two chat windows had popped open even before she could explore the profiles of these guys. *Man, life on the Internet is exciting and hectic. And I've never had so many men chase me at one time!… Okay, let's do this!* Feeling quite like a femme fatale, Naina opened her messages and went through all the profiles.

Let's see…hmm. Wait!

The first message was from someone named Boy-Toy.

> **(12:15 pm) Boy-Toy:** Your profile is interesting. Would you like to be my friend?

The name didn't sound right. And the profile of a young 24-year-old boy 'looking to make friends' just didn't sound like her knight in shining armour.

Arrgh! I specified the need to chat with a man. I definitely do not want to be chatting with someone my son's age, pretending to be 24!

Naina was put off and hit the 'Delete User' button, as she moved onto the next 'suitor'.

Another chat window popped open. This time, it was someone called TrueBlue.

> **(12:19 pm) TrueBlue:** How does somebody as interesting as you not have a boyfriend in your life? Hey... Can I get some discount on the age limit.

TrueBlue seemed like a nice, regular guy, but he was a decade younger than her, Naina knew that she would not connect with him in the future and so... 'Delete User'.

Who do we have next?...

The messages got so entertaining that she cracked up. As the messages progressed, they took a typical pattern of the same questions and comments: 'Would you like to be my friend?' 'Hi. Pretty similar profiles, girlfriend.' 'Chat and...?' 'Hi! Cool username... Want to tempt me?' 'I love the '80s too! Wanna rock with me????'

She went through a whole bunch of profiles to further separate the grain from the chaff, or in other words, the men from the boys.

> **Cupidfindertron**
>
> 40 / M / Straight / Available
>
> Bombay, India
>
> **My self-summary:** Engineering professional with sexy bum... wnkz
>
> **What I'm doing with my life:** Looking around for looove

I'm really good at: Sarcasm, mating with the bells that are dumb and being mild mannered ☺
The first things people usually notice about me: Geeky face on a beefy body

Naina took a look at Cupidfindertron's profile picture. *He's truly beefy. Dumb Jock! Seriously? I take offence to women being referred to as 'dumb bells'! Whatever that means! Not my type.* She pressed the 'Delete User' button yet again.

'Next one, please Lord!' muttered Naina, praying that a profile she would like opened up next.

Spiritual Master

36 / M / Straight / Single

My self-summary: Spirituality is what keeps me going. I seek a spiritual friend. Love is within us, others just become medium to evolve that love and add or extend its dimension. hence searching for love outside or from someone else is just a mirage.

What I'm doing with my life: Looking around for divinity

I'm really good at: Sharing and giving love

The first things people usually notice about me: My peaceful and sublime attitude

I'm really good at: Listening to people and sharing their life ordeals

'Ha ha! He figures that the shortest way to a woman's heart is through her soul! Ciao.' Naina promptly hit 'Delete User'.

At that very time, a chat window popped open and the conversation went straight to, "Hi, let's talk..."

(12:55 pm) Igetyou: What are you looking for?

(12:56 pm) Temptress 007: What am I looking for? Kindness. Someone who doesn't snub me all the time. Just because you turn around and say—Hey, I am a bastard—doesn't make it ok to actually be a bastard. Be a better person! I want a better person.

(12:58 pm) Igetyou: Oh! ok then. I'll leave you to finding the "kindness"

Don't ask if you can't handle it, douche bag! 'Delete User' was pressed yet again.

LesbianLovermania
21 / F / Single / Gay
My self-summary: I m a lesbian and into fems ;) and I m a down to earth person!
What I'm doing with my life: Working and in school :)
I'm really good at: Cooking! Lol!
The first things people usually notice about me: Face boobs hair

Naina was a bit shell shocked at the boldness of this goddess. 'Delete User'.

She shut her laptop. *Enough...* she sighed out aloud. *Why on earth do I need a man to make me feel complete? Why can't I feel at peace by myself? Men are such losers anyway!*

Naina took a break and stepped out from her office room for a cigarette. *Gosh, this place is totally whacked out! It is seriously strange. I mean these people sound deranged. Can't I find a single decent guy to chat with, let alone date? What's become of this world? If this is the quality of men, then God save all the women on this site. Why is it that men today just don't seem to match up with the expectations of women around?* She thought about the people she knew in her life, there were so many interesting, well-balanced women, but so few men like that.

Her thoughts went to Rahul. He had a certain personality. *He has a great personality. If only he would commit to this relationship a bit more. We need to be on the same page.* She thought about the first time she met Rahul. Soon after her divorce, Naina was looking for a job to sustain her kids and herself. She met him through a common friend. Rahul was looking for a manager to look after his affairs and Naina fit the bill. After all, she had looked after a business even when she was married and was used to managing clients and the day-to-day running of a factory. Rahul was going through a messy business transaction and needed an assistant while he was fighting the case in court. Naina had flexible timing, the salary was decent and the office was just a block away from home.

It all sounded perfect till Rahul started to come on heavily. Initially, Naina was a little put off with Rahul's overtures, but with time, she too gave in and they soon became a couple. *The oldest cliché in the book—boss and assistant; both divorced, supporting each other… Jeez!*

Naina often felt that it all happened too fast…maybe, she was a bit vulnerable. She often regretted getting into a relationship with Rahul. Was it her insecurity or just her way of getting back to a 'normal' life? It had been a while now…she had risen fast in the office hierarchy and was managing clients by herself. *At least, I am no longer the cliché of an assistant!*

At home the next day, Naina sat with her laptop open, and pondered, *The Internet seems like a dark place to find the perfect man, if there ever was one who existed.* She was not done with Rahul, but she was dissatisfied with him. Rahul had become her worst habit. She was more troubled by him rather than being happy with him. *I guess the honeymoon phase is over and we are still plodding on with this…whatever this is!*

She wanted mature, real men. There was once a time when men used to be real. When they dressed with style and had a certain 'honour' code that involved treating not only their elders and each other with respect, but women alike. Unfortunately, those days were far gone—a thing of the past. *Ha! It was an era when you didn't even exist, sweetheart!* The ones she had interacted with on *Cupidity*, so far, seemed to ring hollow. *Rahul seems like a dream compared to these guys. These guys are just lame!*

She was a little disheartened. She realised that she was getting hit on by a bunch of annoying kids, who seemed to have pinned her as a 'cougar kill'; sublimating men; stuttering blokes; floppy-haired bores and so on and so forth. She called Tara.

"Hey Nains, what's up?"

"Hi! Got a minute? Are you busy?"

"A little… In the middle of some work. But tell me?"

"Well… I went on the site and I am giving up already."

"No! What do you mean?"

"I don't know how you find people here, it's nothing but pesky little kids or demented souls looking for solace."

Tara was pleased that Naina was giving it a shot at least, "Oh, don't worry! I had a bunch of hits and misses too. You need to tweak your search a bit, and have some patience. Sift out the kids and just hang in there."

Just when she was about to finish her conversation with Tara, a new message popped up in her inbox. Naina opened it. It was from someone named As_seem.

> **(11:45 am) As_seem:** Hi! I happened to trip over ur profile while scrolling the site and found it kinda intriguing. Lol! We share common turf of likes if not dislikes... do go through my profile and if u find more in common then drop me a line.

Normal. Not pushy, thought Naina, as she quickly told Tara about the message. "Tara, I think I want to respond to this one."

"See! Have fun and let me know where it goes."

Naina disconnected the call and explored As_seem's profile.

> **Name: As_seem**
>
> **Age: 39**
>
> **City: Mumbai, India**
>
> **A brief description:** I am crazy, stupid, and charming. I'm not loony or desperate, just adventurous enough to try dating online.
>
> **What are you doing with your life:** When I am not working, I am out with friends and family partying like a 'Rock Star'. I have an old neglected acoustic guitar. I like playing her whenever I have the time.
>
> **List a few of your favourite things**
>
> The Gym and Biking, music and travel, gizmos and cars.
>
> **Books:** Articles, Blogs, Books, Sci- Fi and DIY... I read anything and everything

Movies: Action / horror flicks

Food: I'm an all-out foodie... I haven't met a dish I haven't liked ;-)

The first thing someone notices about you: My smile, I got lucky with the dimples ladies (thanks mom and dad!)

Things you could never do without: My freedom, my cigarettes, brewed coffee with pancakes for breakfast!

What do you spend most of time thinking about: What women want...

What is a typical Friday night for you: Drinks with friends, a meal, a weekend getaway... anything... I'm done by the weekend.

The most private thing you are willing to admit: Cool guys make it first.

Who should contact you: Straight, Single, Normal Women. I hate peroxide hair and bottoxed lips. Ideally between 35-45, with no deep embedded chip on their shoulders. I'm a simple guy... attitude confuses me.

People should message you if: If you are single, sexy, smart, fit and fun... Enthusiastic about life's small things—a good laugh, or even better, great conversation over a meal... and let's face it, we are on a dating site, so intimacy definitely.

Naina decided she liked what she read and responded to his message.

(12:30 am) Temptress 007: Actually, I came on this site just for a lark and decided to choose the boldest, craziest name possible! I wanted to be a tease, get a rise... figuratively. The Temptress is my fantasy; wish I could be like her all the time!

(12:35 am) As_seem: You seem like someone out on a hunt... with that extra spice, a la Bond 007. Lol! Tell me, what makes you take on such a name— Temptress 007.

After sending in her reply, Naina relaxed. She decided to stick on the chat and play along. It was a welcome distraction from making Rahul the centre of her existence. She liked As_seem's confidence, his quick wit and the fact that he seemed like a 'normal' guy. Just when Naina was about to reply to his message, a chat window popped up on the bottom end of the page.

(10:00 pm) As_seem: Hey! lets chat online on the messenger chat window. more convenient
(10:03 pm) Temptress 007: hi Aseem, yes, I like this. It's easier to chat on this window
(10:03 pm) As_seem: Nice meeting u Temptress. Haven't had such sweet temptation of late, lol!

(10:04 pm) Temptress 007: Really? Thanks, you flatter me.

(10:04 pm) As_seem: So here I am... Ready to succumb to the charms of the temptress.

(10:08 pm) Temptress 007: Look, who is out for the kill tonight!?

(10:15 pm) As_seem: I have a friend who told me tht she could corrupt any saint... and i kinda dropped dead laughing. I thought she was the ultimate temptress. I didn't know she had competition.

(10:16 pm) Temptress 007: In a population of a few odd billions, u didn't think u'd meet her match on this planet?

(10:17 pm) As_seem: Ha ha! So let's play out your fantasy. Actually, it is sheer pleasure meeting the temptress... most women want to be the blessed virgin, born to immaculate conception.

Naina quickly checked out his profile picture. He stared back at her in a candid shot lounging on a recliner. He looked rather handsome; tall, fair, dark hair, brown eyes and a dimpled smile that made you go *Oooohhhh!* It was safe to assume that she was rather tickled by the bonus of his looks.

He's 39! Perfect! No wonder he can hold a conversation with me. In real life, Naina was aware of her divorcee status and always underplayed her charms. She was careful not to give men the wrong signals. Based on her recent past experiences, it didn't take too much for men, especially the old farts, to take any gesture and call it a 'signal'. But tonight, on this website, she let her reigns loose.

(11:10 pm) Temptress 007: So... how does fun play out with you?

(11:10 pm) As_seem: I play board games... Ha ha! Seriously though. Well, you know... Hang out with friends, go to movies, eat at restaurants. Clubbing sometimes...

(11:13 pm) Temptress 007: Sometimes is how frequently... u mean every day?

(11:14 pm) As_seem: Yeah, well. Not that much...

(11:14 pm) Temptress 007: Just four days a week.

(12:00 am) As_seem: No! Maybe a couple times a month; that's it!

(12:01 pm) Temptress 007: Ya Ya . sure, I believe you. You probably know every bartender and doorman there.

As_seem, or Aseem as he was called beyond the virtual world, confessed that he was only a three-month-old entrant to the online dating game and wanted to test waters first. He was curious to see how the 'mating game' worked online. After they chatted for a while, she figured that Aseem was from Mumbai and was an importer dealing in imported products for the hospitality industry. He seemed well travelled. Work took him all over the world and there was certain sophistication about his persona. 'Naughty and quirky.' What Naina also liked about him was that he liked to live life passionately and on the edge. He also had a way of teasing her and drawing her out of her shell. She had to admit that she was beginning to enjoy herself.

Over the next few days, Naina got comfortable and familiar with the online world thanks to this guy. She renamed him 'Cliffhanger' because he was exciting and edgy; he radiated this rush of adrenaline as if he was 'hanging off a cliff'. He seemed to be a man around town, and like all people on this platform, carried on a conversation with an air of boldness.

After the tiring intensity with Rahul over time, and the consistent lows that she was increasingly experiencing, her conversations with Aseem were a welcome change. It was light-hearted and fun. They would typically catch each other at lunchtime. The random conversations kept them hooked.

It was a Friday afternoon and they had been engaged in chat sessions all week long. Intrigued by her 'temptress-on-a-prowl' persona, he probed further.

(1:34 pm) Cliffhanger: I had been meaning to ask you... What's an attractive woman like you doing without a guy? You should have scores of men hitting on you

(1:35 pm) Temptress 007: Ha ha! Far from it. There seems to be a real drought of men. Here of course, you are the exception.

(1:35 pm) Cliffhanger: Of course i am ;)

(1:37 pm) Cliffhanger: So are you seeing someone?

(1:37 pm) Temptress 007: Hmm! Tough to say... i am... Well, i don't even know if I can call it that... 'in a relationship'.

(1:38 pm) Cliffhanger: Clearly some problem there or else you wouldn't be here on a dating site chatting with me. Just to have you on the same page, I am currently very single.

(1:38 pm) Temptress 007: How come?

(1:39 pm) Cliffhanger: i'm out of a long relationship and deeply appreciate my singlehood.

(1:39 pm) Temptress 007: what happened?

(1:40 pm) Cliffhanger: It's a long story... let's leave it for another day.

Naina was secretly relieved after she told him and also secretly pleased to know that he was 'very' single. There was no reason to hide her relationship status from Aseem. She liked the fact that he was still interested in her despite Rahul and didn't probe into it more than she revealed. It was a sign of a mature man. Naina enjoyed talking to Aseem. She was open with him and he appreciated that. She voiced her inner thoughts to him. The more she interacted with Aseem, the deeper the comparison with Rahul became for her. Aseem was considerate and Rahul was full of himself. Aseem made her feel significant.

Naina was totally intrigued, and there was a little voice in her head that kept saying, "Hey, this guy is nice." To believe in 'Mr. Nice' at this point felt just about as silly as believing in Santa Claus, but there was a certain draw about being online with him. Plus, he was upfront too and completely straightforward. She didn't feel like she was being taken for a ride.

The conversations carried on over the next few days. She got to know more about Aseem. He had grown up with three sisters, so he wasn't alien and awkward around women. He claimed he understood the significance of communication for women and how most of them longed for it in a relationship. Naina thought of Tara and how her lack of connect with Ranvir had led her to the website. *Well, it isn't the only reason, but it is a major reason,* she thought.

Naina was amazed at how quickly this guy, all the way down in Mumbai, wanted to *see where this went.*

(2:07 pm) Cliffhanger: so tell me… wht makes u stay in a relationship that's, hmm, at best iffy

(2:08 pm) Temptress 007: I dunno?

(2:08 pm) Cliffhanger: Ok, well, why are you in a relationship that's not ok? Why not find one that's amazing?

(2:08 pm) Temptress 007: There aren't any such relationships

(2:09 pm) Cliffhanger: U mean u r scared to play the part, run with the hare and hunt with the hounds

(2:09 pm) Temptress 007: ;)

(2:09 pm) Temptress 007: the temptress doesn't hunt, she simply lures

(2:10 pm) Cliffhanger: Who is this super bold flirt? I like her, already!

She rolled her eyes and diverted the conversation. *Online chatting does enhance your sense of intimacy,* observed Naina who had her walls down with Aseem now. It felt wonderful. She definitely did not expect to be so candid in 10 days of chatting with some stranger. *This is a tease; really,* she thought one afternoon. Her life was at changing point. Naina could feel it, but still did not want to give too much importance to her online tête-à-têtes.

The conversations flowed into a deeper note:

(1:25 pm) Cliffhanger: Hey! btw, I don't know what brought you here. I am just glad you made it... ;)

(1:29 pm) Cliffhanger: for me black is black, and so is white... Problem is I can't find much of grey areas in life

(1:30 pm) Temptress 007: Thr is no room for grey?

(1:30 pm) Cliffhanger: There is room for grey, but usually I don't find myself landing on that part too much.

(1:30 pm) Temptress 007: I totally am on board with the grey areas. I feel black and white are very dull perspectives. I'm screwed! Ha ha!

(2:11 pm) Cliffhanger: well I have been so engrossed in work... for all the odd and even reasons, but now I choose to be on this site to take control of my personal life...

(2:12 pm) Temptress 007: I think this is my way... this harmless banter... to retaliate to Rahul's crazy womanising ways. Not that I am seeking revenge...

(2:13 pm) Cliffhanger: So, what do you do?

(2:14 pm) Temptress 007: I work in a relocation company, mostly relocating expats

(2:14 pm) Cliffhanger: You like it?

(2:15 pm) Temptress 007: Hmm! It's ok. I like the job but not sure about the boss

(2:16 pm) Cliffhanger: ok, well, why are you doing a job that's just ok? Why not find one that's amazing?

(2:17 pm) Temptress 007: Lol! There are no amazing jobs.

(2:18 pm) Cliffhanger: There's got to be an amazing job... an amazing one... somewhere out there

Naina loved his idealism and straight-from-the-heart feel that this guy exuded. She loved Rahul, but she liked the person that Aseem was. She resolved in her head, *I will just chat, that's about it.* She was simply not going to cross the line... *It can't be this easy,* she thought, *it's never been so easy... being swept away is a thing in books and movies! Anyway, just stop over-analysing.* For now, all she knew was that it was exciting and that she was hooked.

(2:23 pm) Cliffhanger: Back to work! Lassie, u gotta lotta work to do today, so, stop daydreaming!

3

Going Nutty

It was July, the rainy season had set in and Delhi was at its greenest best. Tara's misadventures with Pepper & Salt happened. Tara had found nobody riveting enough to get her online fix. She was hesitant to go on the site but she was seriously bored. The website was like a virtual candy store, with so many different types of candy up for the taking. Although she had many messages in her inbox, she seriously did not find anybody worth responding to.

Tara had logged in after a few days and started going through a lot of profiles. Tara's patience with finding someone right on *www.cupidity.in* was running thin. She sighed, *I'm getting hit on by kids, a gigolo and a bisexual who all are professing undying love. Why can't someone be cool enough to just chat?* She had almost given up on meeting somebody interesting to chat with. There was one profile that caught her eye, though. It was of a 45-year-old whose chat name was 'Nuttyasauras.'

PROFILE

Name: Nuttyasauras

Age: 45

City: New Delhi

A brief description: A question mark on a tabula rasa

I'm really good at: Being needlessly verbose and pointless. I think most things are absurd and I am not arrogant enough to assume that the same is not true for me.

The first things people usually notice about me: My grumpy look, the vacant stare. the poisonous fangs. And before it's too late… they notice the horns and the 666—mark of the Satan.

List a few of your favourite things: I can't read. Am severely dyslexic. Peep shows remain a clear favourite. I love the Kenny G they play in toilets. It's like the magic combination of smooth jazz, pee and crap odours.

Things you could not do without: I have a kit with some precision surgical scalpels for the administration of torture. I end by getting my victim to inhale laughing gas. For the unlisted esoterica, contact me!

What do you spend most of your time thinking about: Imponderables. I am working hard on the unified theory—to link classical and quantum physics. I think string theory is bunkum, though I love g-strings!

What is a typical Friday night for you: Planning the witches' Sabbath. My responsibilities include brewing potions and ensuring that no one disturbs the peace of the naked witches doing the jig.

Who should contact you: Single women who like men. Ideally between 30 and 45 years of age. Anyone up for making new friends, or looking for long-term dating, even short-term dating, or just activity partners.

People should message you if: Other than tight-assed *behenjis*, all are welcome. I find bigots, zealots, chauvinists, jingoists, those on the far right of the political spectrum, believers in astrology, numerology, neo-age cults, believers in past life regression, wannabe proselytisers of old religions and in general, batty, irrational and bitchy women very repulsive. But of course all caveats are waived off for hot women. I believe... um... er... my romantic love will change them for the better.

Interesting! Very witty! His profile got her tickled. *But before I go any further…what does he look like?* This time round she asked for a picture first. *Hmmm…attractive, boyish, fit. Quite dreamy and intense.* She liked what she saw.

(08:10 pm) Ubercool: Are you busy?

(08:10 pm) Nuttyasauras: no not at all

(08:11 pm) Nuttyasauras: am randomly surfing

(08:11 pm) Nuttyasauras: reading crap

(08:12 pm) Ubercool: What are you looking for in here

(08:12 pm) Nuttyasauras: :)

(08:14 pm) Nuttyasaurus: is that a serious question? I really don't know what I'm looking for here, I'll probably find out when I do. But if you're up to talking about nothing in particular, and if you like sitting in prolonged silences, maybe we could chat a little or something

He seemed to be just what Tara was looking for—to hit it off with another intellectual sort. Tara launched into a feisty chat session with Nuttyasauras and was having a splendid time. For the next few hours, she slipped in and out of real and web life. *I love this tongue-in-cheek conversation.*

(9:14 pm) Ubercool: i think i'm one of those who look for constant excitement

(9:14 pm) Nuttyasaurus: get into the secret service

(9:14 pm) Ubercool: you know the ennui sets in

(9:15 pm) Nuttyasaurus: become an assasin for hire

(9:15 pm) Ubercool: want to hire me

(9:16 pm) Nuttyasaurus: you re a softie

(9:16 pm) Nuttyasaurus: interor designer, art curator and pretentious stuff like that.

(9:16 pm) Ubercool: makes money, pays the bills

(9:16 pm) Nuttyasauras: do you run a gallery as well?

(9:17 pm) Ubercool: it's not pretentious by any chance

(9:17 pm) Nuttyasaurus: lol... knew it would irritate you

How do you 'know' already? Tara was intrigued by him.

(9:18 pm) Ubercool: What kind of a place would the world be without the creative arty types... being a philistine like you would be such a dry place to be in

(9:18 pm) Nuttyasaurus: aha!

(9:18 pm) Ubercool: Does this philistine have a name?

(9:19 pm) Nuttyasaurus: the typical bias of the *arty* types. Hi, I am Jai

(9:19 pm) Ubercool: science and creativity are actually two sides of a coin. JAI ho! I am Tara.

Nuttyasauras became 'Nutty' as he went on to entertain Tara for the next few minutes. *Nutty suits you,* she thought.

His inferences from whacked-out-theories-land cracked her up. He teased her with them through the night.

> **(10:20 pm) Nuttyasauras:** Speaking of art... you know that Hitler and Bal Thackeray were both art lovers and despots, right?

Tara had a smile on her face as she chatted away with him. Nutty had her in splits most of the time. She sensed her body shutting down. Despite the fun, she called it a night around midnight. As she got into bed, she thought about her new-found friend, Nutty. *What fun to chat with him...that was all I really needed,* she snuggled up cosily under the Jaipuri blanket. She heard Ranvir's voice in her head, 'Intellectual Masturbation'. *Whatever...*, she thought as she turned to her side and fell into a deep sleep.

As days went by, she hit it off really well with Nutty. She found a patient and reassuring chat friend in him. She found Nutty extremely perceptive and liked the way he got to the point straight. Unlike Pepper & Salt, he was a lot more upfront, he was always forthcoming with information and she got to know about his peeves, his favourites and his dislikes rather quickly. Most people in cyberspace keep their dirty stuff under lock and seal it; Nutty was open to conversation and had no problem in adding her on Facebook and sharing pictures and information about him. Also, he was more her age and a lot more relatable in many ways.

Her interactions with him and the other guy increased as she downloaded the *Cupidity* app on her mobile again.

They were in touch throughout the day. She would catch him before breakfast and between work.

Nutty: PING!

Nutty: whatsup?

Ubercool: Not much, just making a sandwich. I am starving for some reason

Nutty: At 11:30 am? That is a strange time for you. No breakfast today?

Ubercool: Unfortunately not. I was running out of the house with Neil. He had to be dropped at the school because the bus didn't come. Then I just got into errands... how is your day coming along, luv?

Nutty: Now that you called me "luv" it just got better...

Nutty: I know... that sounded way too corny for my sarcastic dark-ish personality. Stop making me sound like sunshine, woman! I like playing the brooding realist. It suits me!

Ubercool: Ha ha ha!... Nutty, I am happy to play "sunshine" to your wicked soul.

She chatted endlessly with Nutty about random things—from routine for the day to Neil and his raging teenage hormones, to discussions on the most moving music symphony, Hitler's managerial brilliance, or even a crack at each other's professions.

Nutty seemed to uplift Tara's spirits. She felt that she knew more about Nutty's life than that of Ranvir's at this point. *What is there to talk about with Ranvir anyway?* Tara just found Nutty so intensely funny and spontaneous that she responded to him effortlessly. They had even exchanged their cell phone numbers but had never called each other as yet.

Tara wanted to sort out her thoughts by voicing them aloud. Over a routine coffee session with Naina, she touched upon the topic.

"Where are you, woman? You seem distracted, but in a peaceful way."

"Ya, you know, these chats with Nutty have been such a welcome change, Nains."

"Yes, I am aware. It seems like 'all-the-time kinda stuff' now. You are engrossed on your phone like some teenager," Naina winked playfully at Tara.

Tara rolled her eyes, *Teenagers!* "I have been thinking about it. As fun as it is, I can't help but draw parallels between my relationship with Ranvir, and this new space with Nutty."

"You are human, you know!" Naina commented between sips.

"I think what draws me to Nutty is that he is flirtatious without being too much in the face of it."

Tara took a sip of her steaming coffee, "He honours me but is not pushy, like, he never insists on meeting up. Also, the anonymity of an online chat suits me just fine. It is perfect and I like the pace and enjoy the chase." She looked at Naina, "But really, everything put aside, Nutty does make me laugh a lot."

She was in a happy place. He seemed to be interested in her and it was uncanny how he peeled away the many layers to get to know her better. She constantly compared him to Ranvir, who was now an emotionally-distant husband. *Not the man I married, definitely not the man I pictured spending my life with!*

"Come on Tara, we all know there is a difference between a long-term relationship and a new-found connect. These are signs of a new connect."

"I know things change in a marriage, Naina. I am not naïve. But it seems that for Ranvir, I am not part of his comfort zone anymore. Hell, I am completely removed from every zone! We are disconnected from each other. Nutty loves to chat, unlike Ranvir who is more of a recluse. With Nutty, I feel alive. And all this attention doesn't hurt."

Sure, it was not fair to compare this short a time with Nutty to a marriage of so many years. But there was an ever-widening gap building between them. Ranvir lived for himself and was unconsciously committed to a detached way of life. And she had voiced it to Ranvir many times. Somewhere in the humdrum of day-to-day life, he stopped connecting with her on a deep, meaningful, and personal level. It is like she became white noise in the background.

It also hurt that she had to make all the compromises and adjustments in their marriage. Her career had to be juggled keeping in mind Ranvir and Neil's needs. They came first in every situation, and she never got any brownie points for giving up on her needs. It always seemed like the done thing. *Taken for granted.* Ranvir always had his way in just about everything. He was free to pack his bags and be up and about, while Tara was left to handle home and hearth. It was finally getting to her. It was no longer the thing that came naturally to her. *I am on the backburner for everyone!* It was an effort to pull everything along solo.

Post dinner, Tara was doing research for a client on her computer. She worked and chatted with Nutty simultaneously.

(10:05 pm) Nuttyasaurus: Am bored out of my skull. Can we please elope or run away? It solves the problem of boredom. Imagine the excitement... Interior designer, art curator, aesthete runs away with a low life, philistine techie. You can teach me about art influence on design: impressionism, expressionism, pointillism—all that crap. And I will educate you about the wonders of science. Your friends will raise a toast to you. Do you see any flaw in this plan?

(10:05 pm) Ubercool: Hmm! ha ha, sounds like a great plan mr irresistible! So when do u offer to take me to kingdom come?

(10:06 pm) Nuttyasaurus: Hey! On second thoughts, what the heck would I do with you, hold your hand and say my prayers? you know you are such a prude within the liberal façade.

(10:06 pm) Ubercool: No way , i m the new buzz in town, I do man, woman and beast

(10:07 pm) Nuttyasaurus: you do nothing of the sort, in fact, you take umbrage at the slightest double entendre

(10:29 pm) Nuttyasaurus: you are a funny bird! You know you have a fling and you get it out of your system... keep it casual

(10:30 pm) Ubercool: NO! But it could be dangerous I don't want any emotional hassles

(10:30 pm) Nuttyasaurus: you are scared of falling in love?

(10:31 pm) Ubercool: No darling!... I am afraid of others falling in love with me. Ha ha ha

Tara knew Nutty well enough to know this was pure boredom conversation, but unwittingly, the thought of running away with him for a naughty weekend seemed rather alluring.

A few days later, Nutty called to say that his friend had a start-up and he had recommended she do the interiors for his office space. He had already fixed a meeting for the next day and casually mentioned that he would be there as well. He nonchalantly ended the conversation with, "Okay then, see you at 11 am tomorrow, we can go for a coffee later, if we have the time."

Tara hung up and immediately dialled Naina. She was a bit anxious to meet Nutty. It felt strange. Somehow an Internet relationship that you keep secret from your husband was not cheating. *Chatting is not adultery, but now, this is taking it to a different level.*

As excited as she was, she admitted to Naina, "I am scared to death. What if the chemistry isn't there? What if it is? What if?... Gosh! A million 'what ifs' are driving me crazy. Post my previous experience, I must have an exit strategy should things not work out."

She was keen to meet the guy she had been talking to for weeks, but emotionally she was a ball of nerves. Naina did what she knew best, be a 'friend' to her friend. She calmed Tara down, "Relax...you have already seen Nutty's photographs. And what you have seen is encouraging enough. It is just a coffee. Go check him out Tara, it's not as though you are going to bed with him. Don't overthink; just go with the flow. Have a coffee."

Naina was right... Tara had quite a definitive picture of Nutty in her mind. She felt a bit reassured, "Maybe you are right. We are on Facebook as well and I have checked out his friends and updates. I know a lot more about his life as compared to Pepper & Salt."

Next morning she woke up before her regular 7 am time. She was a bit nervous. It felt like a date. She went for a shower and while in the bathroom, she let her towel drop to take a good look at herself in the full-length mirror. *Hmm! Everything seems to be in check—hips firm and round, abdomen flat, long unending supple legs and firm, slim thighs.* Her breasts were not as perky as they were even five years ago, but at least they still looked pretty good. Her arms were slim and worked out as she preffered the slightly taut look. Overall, her confidence level went up a few notches. She saw her reflection and said to herself, *It's a freaking coffee, stop checking yourself out. It won't reach that far over a conversation. Dummy!*

She decided to dress smart and professional, yet casual enough for a date. She settled for a blue linen shift dress with flat sandals. Finally in the car, she turned the AC up as the humidity was getting to her. Tara followed the directions that Nutty gave and reached his friend's office just in time. As she pulled her car into the parking, she saw Nutty smoking a cigarette at the entrance. Her first impression of him was, *Rather attractive. Or maybe I am just attracted to him and my bias, mixed with lack of physical intimacy, has changed my standards of attractive.* She rolled her eyes at herself. *Man! You have a gift to overthink. He looks presentable, full stop.*

He saw her and walked towards her. Tall and well built, Nutty was fit and upright. He had a confident gait and an assured way of holding himself. It felt strange to see him face to face for the first time. He was in a white-collared shirt, sans tie, with the top button open and sleeves rolled up. It was paired with grey trousers.

"My buddy is running 30 minutes late. Looks like we do have time for a coffee, after all," he smiled as he led her to the coffee shop.

A bit awkward to begin with, he held open the door for her and walked with her into the building. They didn't have much to say, but Nutty made a real effort to make her feel comfortable all along.

What broke the ice between them was the contrived initial small talk that the two engaged in, while waiting in the queue to order their coffees. After a while, he smiled at her, "You know what? I'm glad I found you on *Cupidity*."

"Really?" She felt more comfortable. This sort of banter was normal for them. "What brought that on?"

"Well, for starters, you are gorgeous, and the bonus—witty and intelligent. Your husband is a fool to leave you alone." His smile widened, "His loss is my gain entirely—a waste of a perfectly good woman! I mean, at least you are normal and that's a lot more than one can ask for in these days of aberrations."

She laughed, "Nutty, flattery could get you quite far! But hey, you only know my side of the story."

"No, I am serious! You are as cool as they come. Trust me. I met up with some four women on this site. All were rather average, regular, boring women. One even turned out to be nuts. I like kinky, but this one was a little over the top. She was a bisexual into BDSM, she wanted me to spank her and then some… She was seriously unhinged, scared the daylights out of me."

His animated style of describing his 'trauma' was truly endearing. The thought of Nutty in BDSM gear, with a leather whip, was so amusing that she was in peals of laughter. They laughed as if they had done this a million times before. She felt completely at home with him. He just had this energy, a devil-may-care attitude and lust for life that was absolutely 'intoxicating'. Tara was accutely aware of the current running through her. When they would break eye contact, they found their eyes sussing each other out. The emotional excitement of meeting each other ran so high that their mechanism became to make conversation flow as randomly as a chat online.

She had a strong reaction to him. *Baby, you are doomed,* she thought to herself as she checked him out while he placed their order.

Twenty minutes later, Nutty's friend walked in apologising profusely for keeping them waiting. Nutty introduced them and excused himself. "Ankush, this is the very talented Tara I mentioned. Tara, Ankush has a plush space in these towers. What? 38th floor?"

Ankush smiled, "Plush? Maybe after Tara is done with it! Right now, it is just an empty space… Yes, on the 38th floor."

"Well, I will leave you to it then. I gotta get back to the office." He smiled and winked at Tara.

A coy smile and a feeble voice, "bye" is all that Tara managed.

Her meeting with Ankush went of well. The office had a magnificent view of the Qutab Minar. This guy knew what he wanted and specified the budget.

This clean-cut thought process makes my work easier, was the first thought Tara had as she headed home. Her mind wandered to the casual yet assured friendship she had witnessed. She got a positive vibe from Nutty. He seemed casual and approachable in his interactions, yet firm and confident as an individual. It gave her the confidence that he did not assume a false identity while chatting; the Nutty she met and the Nutty she spoke to was the same guy. He was as real on any platform.

Later in the evening, Tara called up Nutty to thank him for introducing her to his friend. Nutty said, "Oh! By the way, I like your cool, casual look and your super confident persona. I find myself intrigued by arty babes. Super hot."

"Thank you, Nutty," Tara laughed. "I didn't realise I was being 'assessed' to such a degree." She thought he was cool and that he had lived up to the mental image that she had created of him as well, but felt too shy to tell him. The conversation went to the meeting she had and ended with Nutty threatening, "I will see you again, real soon, babe."

The next two months flew by as they met often. Over countless telephone calls, umpteen coffee and dinner meetings, Tara learnt that Nutty was divorced. He had recently broken up with his wife. He had been hurt, although he never elaborated on the break-up, she did get a sense of a hostile environment. Tara never probed for more. *Hey, when someone doesn't say, I don't ask!* She had huge respect for privacy.

Their conversations were natural, open, honest, direct, funny and often shockingly flirtatious. They told each other things that one would share with a very close friend. He let her in on all his insecurities, stories about his failed marriage and his ex-girlfriends and his friends. She spoke about her lonely marriage, the way things were, and what a harsh contrast that was to the now. They were both emotionally charged. So much of everything came gushing out from beneath the surface. It was natural in this mutually comfortable space.

One day, Nutty and Tara were sitting over a cup of coffee at the mall, located in a posh South Delhi area. They had come out of a movie and were chilling, before getting back home. They were talking about random things and Nutty asked her out of the blue, "Hey, so here is the age-old question! What exactly are women looking for in a man?"

Well, that's an interesting one, yet clichéd. What does a woman want? She laughed, "After the dust of the 20s has settled, you mean? Post the irrational crazy 'lists' put to rest?" She thought for a bit and said, "I think it boils down to a man who she can talk to; a man who is interested in her; a man who is confident, can take charge without being bossy; a man who is 'manly', yet romantic. You know, for women, flowers, gifts and romantic dinners go a long way in building a relationship. It is important for a woman to feel wanted and these gestures are a sign of that."

Nutty looked away, "Now that seems like a tall order, I don't think I'll ever qualify."

She swatted his arm, "Basically, make her feel wanted, dufus!"

Tara looked at him. She had never thought of Nutty in a 'dating' avatar. Strangely, a thought crossed her mind, *He isn't Richard Gere or a George Clooney, but he has a lot of charm that most women would find very attractive.* Nutty had the brains, he was witty and exuded a gentle confidence, a not in-your-face type, but a subtle confidence that every woman would be comfortable with.

Hey, she checked herself, *before you go 'tangoing' into the sunset with him, you better come down to earth. You are a married woman. You can admire, but from a distance.*

Tara felt a bit awkward, she wanted to say, "I do realise there is nothing in store but you are actually the sweetest person to spend one's life with." Instead, she looked at him purposefully, and said, "You are pretty cool, you would make a woman happy one day."

Tara couldn't shirk it off. *Nutty in the date light!* Even though she was married and restrained herself, there was an undeniable chemistry between them. There was a vacuum in her life and she craved for a real connect. She found a combination of intellectual gratification and emotional satisfaction with Nutty.

But here was the quandary. As a married woman, her resolve to circumscribe her overtures were well established. However, now that she was in this new yet familiar space with Nutty, she wanted more. She felt stuck between the devil and the deep blue sea. She knew eventually she would be left wanting for more than just conversation.

She told Naina, "I'm very attracted to Nutty. I certainly agree with the statement that you can love more than one person. I can't find the best word to describe it, but our intimacy is easy and natural. It is not a 'mushy' feeling, it is a great feeling, a...a 'correct' feeling. I now worry about losing him. It is kind of an insecurity that I have developed since the time I have come to know him. I feel deeply for him."

Naina kept quiet. She knew she couldn't have the right-or-wrong conversation with Tara at this point. Nothing would register. *There are times you have to let people live out their own experiences,* Naina thought. "Damn woman... damn," is all what Naina could muster.

One day, while they were strolling in Lodi Garden, Nutty asked Tara about her marriage, "What is going on with you?"

She looked him in the eye and with all the sincerity she could gather, said, "My marriage could have been worse, but it could have been a lot better... We have been married for more than 15 years and have a wonderful son. For all and sundry, we are a happy family. But it's a façade. I remember, all too well, the terrible outbursts of anger I had had over Ranvir's decision to take off for an assignment to Singapore."

"Is this his normal work mode?"

"Now yes... At the time, it was his third assignment away from home and I felt completely abandoned. How I had cried and thrown tantrums, yet, he was adamant and didn't change his mind about taking up offshore work. It's like I didn't count."

"Woman! He gotta 'provide' for you!"

She shook her head, "No Nutty, that is what hurt more. It wasn't about money; we have been blessed with plenty. It was to get away... From me, from Neil...from his own life. What hurt was the realisation that we weren't an entity anymore." Ranvir was a recluse and didn't need her the way she needed him. She looked down, quiet, and kept walking.

Over time, her anger had melted into resentment. Their marriage had hit an all-time ice age. It hurt that he didn't take her into consideration. She gave Ranvir the cold shoulder to say the least, limiting communication to the bare minimum. Nonetheless, she couldn't decide what to do with her marriage. There were very good reasons to call it quits, and there were equally valid reasons to stay and attempt to mend the marriage. Notably, the fact that 'she' still loved him and that he was the father of her son.

"Despite the pain, Ranvir is basically a good man." She still had hope that one day they would be like a normal couple. "I am not willing to write off my marriage. Not yet."

Nutty took her hand as if he understood. They walked towards a monument and sat on a bench facing it. They absorbed the moment in silence, at ease in each other's company—the sunset, a light evening breeze, the smell of freshly-cut grass and the magnificent monument. The moment was surreal. Around them, people walked their dogs, children played, couples and families lounged on the grass. They were surrounded by activity, but there was a sense of calmness about them. They were in a peaceful moment.

He pulled her close and wrapped his arms around her and she put her head on his shoulder. The nip in the October evening air was calming and wrapped in Nutty's arms, she felt comforted. They felt good together and she felt protected and nurtured. Nutty looked at her and lifted her chin gently and kissed Tara. It was a slow, compassionate kiss. Tara turned towards him. She kissed him back. As the passion brimmed, all else faded away in the background. Nothing else mattered. Nutty tasted sweet. There was an urgency that surprised her. It felt natural. She melted into the kiss, deeper and more intense as she leaned into him. She succumbed to his need for her, plummeting into this relationship that was far from simple. It was a defining moment. She had never gone beyond her marriage. Nutty and Tara hadn't given their relationship any name, but this felt like they had jumped several stop lights.

He looked into her eyes, holding her face, "I want you, Tara." She looked sexily dishevelled yet vulnerable. She realised this was turning into something so incredibly real, something she could never have foreseen when she took to chatting online. She kissed him again. She settled into his arms and he rested his cheek on top of her head.

In a while, the moment of truth caught up with her. She had an incisive image of Ranvir flash through her mind. Instinctively, she pulled away. She felt a pang of remorse. But she did not panic. *This is so strange. I should feel guilty, but I don't.* She was a married woman and this was clearly crossing the invisible line. She stayed in Nutty's arms a little longer. She didn't want to move away from this spot. She felt something stir, from deep within her, that hadn't been awakened for far too long. It wasn't about sex, she figured out, she had been feeling numb, lonely and questioning her life. Nutty came in and completed her on an emotional, physical, and spiritual level. He made her feel alive, and while by his side, she found a new lease on life. Finally, she forced herself to get up, dusted herself and said, "Let's go! Neil will be alone at home and I need to help him with his project."

Later, as Tara turned in for the night, she put the thoughts of the evening aside and decided, *Life had a way of sorting things out.* She was truly happy in this space. She was living in many dimensions. Happy to get the companionship she missed with Ranvir, she soaked in all the attention she got from Nutty. For the first time in so many years she wasn't lonely. *For now, I will just live in this moment... I will not think about tomorrow.*

4

Goo-gle! Searched!

There was a slight chill in the air, it had rained in the morning and the air had a clean smell of wet earth. October evenings in Delhi were always pleasant and a respite from the sticky summer heat. She was excited and in good spirits as Ranvir was coming home for the weekend.

Tara was so looking forward to spending time with him. After that brief, yet intimate kiss with Nutty, Tara wanted to reconnect with Ranvir. She felt ensnared by Nutty and in some strange way wanted Ranvir to be by her side. *Maybe this is what guilt feels like...* She could feel that she was slipping into an abyss and wanted to make an effort to save her marriage. She had planned a movie dinner and then some much-needed *action*. Neil was also excited to have his dad home as he wanted to go for the Formula One races in Noida.

Tara had just finished her yoga workout and was just stepping in for a shower when Ranvir called. "Hi, what are you doing? I have some bad news." Ranvir said that he was sorry to disappoint her but his client was flying in and that he wouldn't be able to come for the weekend. Their plans were now kaput as the weekend loomed ahead.

Tara was furious. She started to stride up and down her bedroom. She, who was normally controlled, was seething with indignation. *Darn man! Can't he ever get it? I just crave for 'his' company sometimes. This is like living in a vacuum, I have started to bitterly resent him. What the hell am I to do? I don't have a clue!*

She didn't want to reach out to Nutty every time she felt like this. It was too dangerous. Also, Nutty was travelling for work and was out for a week. *I wish Ranvir and I shared more of our lives together.* She was desperately looking forward to Ranvir's company, to be wooed, to feel young, to feel emotionally in sync, but it seemingly never happened.

The distance between them had been growing in the last few years. Only if Ranvir could be a more involved husband, the draw of the illicit wouldn't be so strong. Nutty was becoming an addiction as heady as cocaine. This must come to an end. Tara took a deep breath and reminded herself of all the reasons that had brought her and Ranvir together. She made a mental note, *Make a list and pin it on your mirror if you have to. Remember the good things about each other, and don't focus on the negatives.*

Tara wondered why it was so difficult for two people to strike a balance. She called up Naina and told her about the last-minute turn of plans. She had too many thoughts that she voiced, "Why are men so oblivious? All I needed was for Ranvir to be involved, be part of my life, not such a stranger? Is that too much to ask? A caring word, some concern, a little understanding, is that so difficult?"

Naina retorted, "Ranvir can turn on his charm with others, it is natural to do so socially. Have you ever tried telling your husband how much you need him to open up to you? Also, Ranvir needs to feel important, respected and needed. Like any man! Have you ever made him feel cherished? You are such a battle axe around him. Ranvir can never be the suppliant husband, Tara. The little that I know about men, if you want more love, give him sex, seduce him and see how things open out for you."

"We have spoken so many times..."

"Maybe you have too many expectations from him. Why don't you just chill...and yes, less conversation and a lot more action, then. Sorry, I have to go for this meeting. You take it easy and don't be so hard on yourself."

As Tara sat there, she thought about what Naina had said. Ranvir always had this air of cold unapproachability about him. Every time she started a conversation with him, she felt she was hitting a stone wall. As time went by she stopped trying and the silences became more intense and painful. For Tara, this total disconnect was palpable, like someone had pulled out a cord from an electric socket. She felt totally uprooted and emotionally troubled with her marriage.

Deep in reverie, the ping of a new message drew her attention to her laptop. The message was from somebody called Goo-gle. A bit tired with her thoughts and with ample time on her hands, she opened the email message in her inbox. It read:

> Hi Ubercool,
>
> I like your profile and would like to be friends with you. I'm a transgender. I am a guy who loves to cross-dress like a chick. I wish I lived in a world where people didn't limit themselves to a box. I am honest, positive, level headed, and looking for like-minded

people who are open to understanding me. I would like to get to know you better.

Goo-gle

She was amazed at how people let down their guard and came out in the open on a chatting site. She reckoned that being online under a pseudonym, people were not afraid to be who they really were. Tara clicked on Goo-gle's profile to know more about him.

PROFILE:

Name: Goo-gle

Age: 25

City: Delhi, India

A brief description: A regular guy or rather the guy next door... a part of me is definitely feminine. I love to cross-dress like a chick and feel more comfortable as a woman. I would love to explore my feminine side... with someone I hope to find here.

Wow! Now that's quite a package. What the heck, let's get a peep into Goo-gle's world... Any which way, he's a lot more interesting than a whole load of soppy men. Tara decided to message him.

(10:07 am) Ubercool: Hi... yeah, I find you interesting... let's chat up

(10:10 am) Goo-gle: Cool... that's what matters really! I am here to meet people who don't freak out when I tell them abt myself...

(10:10 am) Ubercool: I appreciate your honesty... ok, so tell me... what does it mean to be a transgender? Does that mean you are a guy in real but wish to explore your sexuality with a man?

(10:11 am) Goo-gle: Lol... that's far from it. it means that I'm actually a woman in a man's body. I love to dress up like a woman... i identify myself as a woman. i think of myself as a woman and i want to be with a man as a woman. when I dress up, I want to feel like a woman... even sexually. It's just that after living the entire life in a dual mode... my brain is kinda trained to behave like a guy... bt deep down I wld love to be the sexy siren tht I am ;) Unfortunately, people either see me as gay wanting to sleep with other men or as a sex object with a cross-dress quirk. Actually, transgenders are people who are born with a female mind and soul in a male body.

(10:13 am) Ubercool: what happens when you aren't dressed up like a woman? Do you feel like a man? have you done it with both men and women?

(10:13 am) Goo-gle: Well. I have been with women, but as a man. I haven't really been with a guy in a relationship except for a fling I had with my cousin which didn't last for long and was totally physical. I slept with him a couple of times... I loved it... bt I really want to be in a relationship with a man.

(10:15 am) Goo-gle: With women, it is more like an emotional connect... a friendly one... more like a non-sexual one. when i see an attractive woman, as much as I want to be like her, I cannot feel any sexual attraction towards her. my attraction for women is most definitely emotional...

(10:16 am) Ubercool: This is such a different world... go on

(10:16 am) Goo-gle: haha... yes, it is. It may all seem amusing... but i really haven't had much of an experience when it comes to sex... apart from my cousin. i don't have any other experience with men. Yes, i am open to anal sex... i think i actually crave for it... Have your ever had it? it is painful i am sure

(10:16 am) Goo-gle: Shit! i may sound like a crazy person, but i just want to open up to someone and be completely honest

(10:17 am) Ubercool: You make my head spin... following u man-woman / woman-man / man-man / woman-woman... WOW! what an exciting life you have, I can barely handle man-woman!

Tara found all this pretty bewildering. She wondered how strange it would feel to be in conflict with her own sexuality. She thought of what Goo-gle had said, *Transgenders are a 'birth failing', not a life choice. It's an 'anomaly'...like a female mind in a male body.*

Tara forgot all about her own life and tried to slip into Goo-gle's life. His name was Nihal, a 25-year-old regular guy, who looked like a man, but deep within, was a woman. He had a regular job, his family saw him as a man, his friends knew him as a man, but he knew himself as a woman. His only way to identify with himself was when he dressed up as a woman and that's when he felt complete. Nihal lived a closet life.

He was troubled about his existence and was at the crossroads, unable to decide how to move forward. The painful part for Nihal was that his parents didn't know he was a woman in a man's body. The only person who understood him was his sister. He borrowed her clothes to cross-dress. Most of Nihal's relationships had been with women; however they all broke because he wanted to be with a man.

In his mind, Nihal had no doubt that he wanted a sex-change operation. He was just unsure about letting his parents into his real life. His dad was fairly conservative and Nihal was sure he wouldn't take kindly to the decision of going in for a sex reassignment surgery. Somewhere in the back of his mind, he was convinced that his mother knew and understood Nihal's predicament. But she was too scared to acknowledge it and take it up with his father.

That's a lot on his plate. Uff…life must be tough for this kid. His world is so different from mine, my problems seem so unimportant in front of his.

Tara allowed an ironic smile to flit over. She found it easier to connect with Goo-gle than with Ranvir. With Goo-gle it felt it was so easy to just talk, listen, and be heard. Throughout the day, on and off, Tara chatted with Goo-gle to know more, understand more about his life. Post dinner, before hitting the bed, she logged in for a quick chat.

(10:18 am) Goo-gle: Hey, it's my turn now, I want to know more about your life now. problem in your relationship?

(10:19 am) Ubercool: What makes you think I have a problem?

(10:19 am) Goo-gle: Well… you are here, aren't you?

(10:20 am) Ubercool: Hahaha!… you got me there!

(10:20 am) Goo-gle: What made you come to Cupidity?

(10:20 am) Ubercool: My husband is always away for work…

(10:20 am) Goo-gle: And you are bored? Lonely?

He was bang on.

(10:21 pm) Ubercool: How can I define boredom? if I tell u im not looking for sex would that surprise u?... I am here... I am married and on the surface, all seems like... well, like any marriage. Sure, I am married but that doesnt mean I am secure and happy

(10:21 pm) Goo-gle: Most women who come here are looking for an emotional connect, something that's missing in their marriages... I just generally asked on a lighter note

(10:23 pm) Ubercool: How could you figure that out? we have just barely started chatting?

(10:23 pm) Goo-gle: I just feel so sensitive towards women, I seem to understand them completely and I know what it means to feel lonely. I'm also restless looking for that something and somebody

The anonymity of an online friend made her come clean. With him she had no fear of being judged and she let him have it all.

After that, Nihal would often message late in the evening after work and chat about all and sundry. He was adorable, but his world was so bizarre. *Leading parallel lives is so taxing on the mind, body and heart,* Tara thought.

She found a pattern in her conversations with Nihal. They always started on a happy note and then looped into the anger and stress that Nihal felt at having to conceal his identity from the world. On one side, he led a normal 'male' existence, going to work, interacting like a man and dressing up like one. But the frustration of that would build up making him react like a naked wire—the smallest thing would lead to an overreaction. He lived in a never ending loop of shame, anger, frustration and guilt. Tara was beginning to become a regular in the chat room with Goo-gle.

One day, Tara was drumming her fingers impatiently on the laptop keys. *Where the hell is Goo-gle! I'm becoming an addict, but if I go off the site, I'll get bored and then I will want to come back to the Internet... Is there any advice on how to stop my Internet addiction? Does anyone know ways how I can stop being addicted? Somebody help!* Finally, Goo-gle appeared on chat and cut her soliloquy.

(09:13 pm) Ubercool: where have you been?

(09:14 pm) Goo-gle: Life sucks. Let's both run away... a transgender and a hapless married woman, maybe that would make Ranvir jealous! I could always pretend to be your ardent lover.

(09:14 pm) Ubercool: Hahahahaha

Goo-gle, aka Nihal, had a great sense of humour and he managed to make her laugh. Nihal too found comfort in talking to Tara. He was troubled about his dual existence. In his mind, he had no doubt that he wanted a sex-change operation.

(09:15 pm) Goo-gle: I don't know how my folks will react...

(09:15 pm) Goo-gle: anyway... same old... Do you have somebody that you have found here?

Goo-gle was a great shrink and would help Tara speak out. She was scared to admit that she was looking for someone to fill up the empty space in her life, to hang out with and who was fun to be with. It was with him that she first verbalised her thoughts.

> **(09:15 pm) Ubercool:** I have met a guy on Cupidity... I like him a lot, we talk a lot, meet up, go for walks, coffee and stuff, but, I don't know what my future with him is about. At the moment, I'm just enjoying all the attention I get from him and it makes me feel alive all over again. I enjoy the small things with him like just laughing together, going for long walks and the great conversations. I don't need a sleazy rumble between the sheets... I need company... see... You get it, right? But m walking a thin line and I need to take it easy. The draw of meeting him is so strong that I find it difficult to stay away... I am not a fool to think that he won't want more after some time... but I don't want to cheat on... Oh! forget it!...
>
> **(09:16 pm) Goo-gle:** Hmm! I see, you like him, don't you?
>
> **(09:16 pm) Goo-gle:** Its natural you are looking for something that's missing in your marriage.

Tara was relieved about being honest and not having to hear some moralistic bullshit that most of her friends would have had to offer.

Sometimes I feel like running away and leaving all this behind...but I don't have the guts to rock the boat.

Next day, she told Naina the same thing she said to Nihal, "I cannot seem to stay focussed on my marriage. I keep drifting away. And I'm kind of having this emotional relationship with another man. I am forcing myself to stop…I want my marriage to work. But I want my husband to be more responsive. I feel so confused…"

"Stop being so hard on yourself, Tara. You are aware of the lines you want to draw… Hence, you'll be fine."

"Ya…you are right."

A few days later, Tara and Naina were hanging out together at Tara's house. Earlier in the day, they had both gone shopping to the glitzy new mall that had opened in Gurgaon. Everything was on sale and the two friends had a blast together indulging in retail therapy to lift their spirits. They were trying out all their new accquistions. Tara had worn a new black Zara dress and had put on her heels and a bright red lipstick. Naina had bought a new pair of jeans and a white buttoned-down shirt. They were both strutting around and feeling mighty pleased with themselves. Tara said, "Let's chat with Goo-gle. It's time you met him, he's a real doll. I'm sure you two will get along like a house on fire!"

She messaged him and got a reply back instantly, "What a coincidence! I was just going to call you!"

Tara didn't waste a minute and quickly dialled his number. "Hi!… Wait, I am putting you on speaker; Naina is here as well."

Cordial introductions done and after the initial pleasantries, Naina suggested to Goo-gle, "Why don't you come on Skype and chat?"

He said he was dressed up at the moment like a woman and would want to meet them as a woman. Tara agreed on the condition that she wouldn't have to reveal herself on video. She wasn't comfortable with it. Naina, who was a real technology whiz, promptly set up the software and disabled the video camera.

Nihal appeared online and the two friends were bowled over—they almost fell off the bed.

"Hi Ubercool and Temptress! I'm Niharika… It's a pleasure to meet you."

At five feet eight inches, slim and fair with thick cascading shoulder-length brown hair, Niharika aka Nihal was wearing a dress—a blue fitted tunic that reached just above his knees. His neckline showed a perfect cleavage. He had worn loads of bangles and long earrings. He walked towards the screen with a comfortable swagger in his stilettos. Nihal had paid attention to every detail—the artificial nails, lashes and red lipstick all screamed, *I'm a woman and I love being one. I'm sexy! So super sexy!*

Tara was so surprised to see this incredibly young, sensuous woman staring at her that she was completely taken aback by the unexpected. The lines of the famous song, 'She's A Maneater,' by Hall and Oats drifted into her head—*'Oh Oh! Here she comes. Watch ya boys, she'll chew you up! She's a maneater!'*

"Nihal, I mean Niharika! Oh my god! You are so damn beautiful; I can't believe this is for real. What a pleasure to meet you," Tara said.

Naina said, "I almost feel inadequate as a woman in comparison! I'm seriously envious and look at those boobs! How the fuck are they so perfect."

Nihal laughed. "Thanks sweetheart! I would love to have seen you too but that's okay. I can wait for that when you are ready. My boobs are padding honey, till I get the real ones!

I wanted to completely vamp it up, trying to correct the little mistake god made when he created me."

"Ha, Ha," Tara laughed, "you are…such a 'real' woman. I would never have guessed that you weren't! In fact, you are a gorgeous woman!"

Nihal described how he had been perfecting the art of dressing like a diva since he was in the 10th grade. While other boys would complain about dressing in tights and wear make-up for school functions, Nihal would enjoy it immensely.

"I could hardly wait to get into the costume! Into adulthood, I tried to 'be a man' by doing what I considered 'manly'—abusing, playing soccer, PS3. But my efforts to be 'macho' were so boring to me, I tell you! From the time I hit puberty, I was sure I was a girl. I didn't have role models for these feelings."

Both the ladies watching Niharika 'aww-ed' in unison.

"Oh, sweethearts, you two! I went on the Internet to try and figure out what was wrong with me. I didn't even have the word for it then, you know," Nihal air quoted 'transgender.' I tried my best to suppress my feelings, hoping they would just go away. But I refused to confide my deep, dark secret to anyone until *Cupidity*."

"Well, it's time for that change, isn't it?" Tara exclaimed. "You are so feminine, petite and sensuous. You were meant to be a woman. How come you don't have much hair? You are pretty '*chikna*'."

Nihal looked down at himself in a self-check mode, "You think so? Already? Wow! I have been taking hormones to stop hair growth. I am on the hormone treatment, which suppresses the male hormone and its resultant characteristics such as a deep voice and excess body hair for a few months now. It hasn't been long. I can't bear to see hair on my face!"

"You are a natural, Niharika," Naina said.

"When I dress up like a woman, I feel human… I feel like a sexy doll! Ha ha! It's at times like this when I feel most at peace. The real 'me' I'll ever be!" She air-kissed the screen.

"I just air-kissed you back," Tara said.

"I like being a woman and would love to go on a date with a man and be pampered and loved." Nihal twirled as if he were a princess and then came close to the camera and whispered, "You know, my attraction for men is sexual. I mean I would love to make men happy by satisfying them; looking at them, while blowing them; to see the pleasure in their eyes. I would love to be fucked like a bitch—oooo ahh! Ha ha ha!"

Nihal said he had been with men and women. His experience with women was unpleasant to say the least. "I knew right away that this was not for me."

Chatting on a video was so much more engaging. Tara and Naina were sitting glued to the screen like a bunch of teenagers watching porn for the first time.

"And what about men?" Tara asked.

"Well, I haven't really been in a relationship with a guy. I had a fling, with my cousin… as I told you before. But I really want to be in a relationship with a man now."

"Well, it is time, Niharika," encouraged Naina.

"I love your encouragement, Temptress. Unfortunately, reality is more complicated. I haven't met a lot of people who I have connected with…it is a little difficult for people to understand things about me while I hide behind this secret. So although I don't really blame anyone, I am aware that life is not easy for a transgender in India. Most transgenders are ill-treated and harassed. I don't want to be in the closet, but I don't have the guts to come out..."

"Come on, you are who you are!" Naina cut in.

Nihal continued, "Yes. And even if I were to just go for a complete change, it would kill my parents. I don't want them to be the butt of ridicule; our society is so harsh." He sweeped his hands up and down the length of his body, "and so, the show must go on!"

Naina encouraged, "Niharika, you need to be who you are, and the world will finally accept it."

Tara couldn't get over the dual existence. *How strange... man by day, woman by night.* When he dressed like a man he was man; when he dressed like a woman he became a woman. She thought for a bit and said, "Why don't you tell your parents? Get them on board. They will help you."

Nihal sighed. "I have played this out many times in my head, darling! My dad is a typical Indian male. I don't think he will be able to take in a shocking news like this. Hahahaha, he'd probably have a movie-style heart attack."

"Come on...I am sure they want you to be happy. Try! You would be surprised. As a parent, I know one thing for sure—all you want is for your child to be happy. And even though you might get hurt over something, you get over it because it's your child for Pete's sake!"

"Yes...deep within, I know I gotta get my life in order."

Naina took the cue to change tracks, "One thing is for sure. You, sweetheart, have such a distinct style. It would be interesting to get tips from her, isn't it Tara?"

Nihal knew more about all the girlie stuff than Tara and Naina did. They thought of going shopping with him and dressing up together. They actually started to mull over the idea to meet up in person.

Then on, life was rocking for Tara. Between Nutty and Nihal, Tara had all the excitement she could handle in her life. Nutty gave her all the attention that Ranvir was unable to give her. He made her feel like a woman, wanted and special. She wasn't ready to give this up. Not yet. *It feels so freakin' delicious!*

With Nihal, it was a picnic. They had conversations on everything under the sun. He was like a long-lost friend and they just couldn't stop talking.

One day, out of the blue, Nihal told Tara that he would be getting off the *Cupidity* site as he thought the site was very dangerous and a waste of time. Tara could sense that something had happened, but he was holding back from her. "Why are you sounding so distant?"

Tara could sense that he was shutting down and withdrawing into his own shell. Something was killing him, it was a new story. She feared it brought him to a breaking point and she was scared that he was hurting badly.

Finally he told her what happened.

He had been chatting with a guy on *Cupidity*. This had been going on randomly for over a month. He liked him and was attracted to him, and had opened up to him. He was transparent about being a transgender. He had also video chatted with him as Niharika and the guy seemed very interested in meeting him. Nihal, dressed as Niharika, had gone on a coffee date with him that morning. After a cup of coffee, the guy invited her over to his place.

Nihal sounded really upset, "At first, I hesitated, but the guy seemed genuinely chilled about it. He told me that he liked me and that he wanted to spend the day with me."

When they reached his place, he immediately pounced on Niharika and started kissing her, "Almost violently! He then pushed me on the floor and started pulling off my clothes and tried to have sex, forcefully!"

"The desperation in the guy…I knew I had gotten myself into trouble. I said no and tried to leave." When Niharika tried to resist, the guy got so angry, he hit her, kicked her and started abusing her.

Tara felt sorry for her friend, "Oh sweetheart…"

Apparently, that guy called him a 'hijra' and told him that no normal man would want to have a relationship with him in his right mind. "Tara, he was screaming at me like a mad man. He said, 'Which man would want to touch you? You are an abnormality. Get out, you ugly freak!' I ran out of there. I felt deeply ashamed and very ill. I feel so dirty right now."

Tara knew that Nihal was badly hurt and would withdraw into his own shell. The angst in him was killing him. He was feeling humiliated and all his insecurities were brimming up. "Will I ever have a normal relationship…no man will ever take me seriously. Why do people hate me?"

"Hush…one asshole cannot be equated with everyone. Don't do this to yourself!" Tara panicked at the thought of losing him. She explained calmly, "People behave like this because they are insensitive, cruel and ignorant. Bottom line, it is their own insecurities that show up when they react like animals. The issue is not really with you but with themselves."

"You are right. He is an asshole. Who behaves like this? Savage!"

"Exactly! Look, how about we meet up in person? I really want to meet you. How about meeting me at the Gymkhana? It's close to your place and you can pop in. I'll ask Naina to join us. Come on, you will feel better. I promise! Whenever it suits you..."

He reluctantly agreed to meet soon.

Later that evening, Tara tried to lift his spirits as she was scared of losing a friend. She implored over a message:

> Hey,
>
> I'm super excited about meeting you. Are you aware that you are one of the most interesting persons I've met in my life? You make my head spin... I want to talk to 'you' so much. So see me soon. Pleeeasee!!!!

Nihal was in no mood for conversation, but begrudgingly agreed. Tara didn't want to push him or her luck any further.

5

Unexpected Exception

It was Friday evening. It had been an extremely hectic week at work with the festive season kicking in. As Naina walked into her apartment, she kept her laptop bag on the dining table. Immediately, she heard a 'ping' on her *Cupidity* app. She smiled to herself, knowing very well that it was Aseem's usual logging in time.

As_eem: Hey… What is the pretty lady doing tonight?

Temptress 007: Well, actually just got in from work… Why, handsome? Do you have plans for me tonight?

As_eem: Well… ya… I could. Want to go for a candlelight dinner with yours truly?

Temptress 007: Don't shit me, dude! :-O

As_eem: Try me… I could be at your doorstep in 15 minutes.

Temptress 007: Ha ha!… You got some sort of travel machine? Or a Concord?

As_eem: I'm serious… Test it out?

Temptress 007: ok, let me take a bet on it. 15 minutes. my place. w-540, gk Block 3. Landmark: opposite Gold's gym.

As_eem: See you soon, sweetheart!

It was close to half an hour that Naina had had the chat with Aseem. She had changed into comfortable slacks and an old, faded pink tee. As she settled back into her recliner, the doorbell rang. *You are shitting me*, Naina thought.

She opened the door and gasped. There he was, leaning against the side of the door casually. Even then, he was a head taller than her. Aseem looked as charming as he did in his photographs with his light-hazel eyes, dimples, and a strong square jawline.

"Are you serious? Aseem!?"

"Hahaha," He winked, "I wasn't kidding!"

Naina's heart skipped a beat. He wore a warm smile and looked dapper in his jeans and a white shirt, *Simple. Smart. Casual,* she thought.

He had soft brown tousled hair. She immediately liked what she saw. He presented her with a lovely bunch of lilac and white petunias.

"Lady, your date is here! Your chariot awaits."

"I'm not ready to go out."

"Come on, you got ten minutes…though I don't care… You'll look gorgeous even in a sack… Finally we meet, Temptress. May I say, it has been worth the wait."

"I don't know what to say… This is all so…"

"Sudden? Yes, I figured this is the only way to do this… Are you going to invite me in?"

"Ha ha! Sorry… I am just at a loss for words. Hi Cliffhanger, I am happy to finally meet you too. Come on in… Let me quickly get dressed."

Fifteen minutes later, Naina stepped out for dinner with Aseem. She wore a cool, casual grey-and-white dress.

They went to a new Italian joint that was perfectly cosy for a first date.

Aseem asked, "So, if we were not out together right now, what would you be doing?"

"I don't know…umm…reading, listening to music, or maybe… just watching porn!"

"My kinda girl!"

Naina laughed, "A dream girl for any man, actually. What would you be doing?"

"Jerkin' off to the same porn, I guess!"

This broke the little bit of awkwardness there was between them. They had a grand time—with so much to talk about, there wasn't any dull moment. They caught up with 30 odd years of each other's lives.

Aseem was in town to bid for a piece of land for the firm he worked for. He had just been made a partner and this was his first big deal.

"When I was 10, my uncle brought me a bag full of football memorabilia from the UK. I would get him to bring me T-shirts, cards, caps and sling bags. I would then sell them to my friends at twice the cost. And I was the richest of the 'pocket money gang' at school."

"So you have always been ambitious?"

"Ya… But I have many different 'passions' to pursue." He winked while he stressed on the 'passion' bit.

As the conversation progressed, they discovered that they had a lot in common. Aseem was very sporty and Naina loved the outdoors too.

"There is this great bucket list experience. You up for adventure, Cliff?"

"What might that be?"

"There is a paragliding camp by a European company in Dharamshala. Are you up for it? Would you like to go? Apparently, the Dhauladhar range is one of the best gliding sites in the world."

"That sounds fantastic! Let's do it some time."

Aseem was so easy-going that it seemed too good to be true. *Rahul, in comparison, is such a bore.* There was a spark in him that excited her. The evening had a magical air to it. It was almost like they were devouring each other's past lives.

Aseem questioned her about her 'in-a-relationship' status. She found herself reluctant to talk about Rahul. A sudden wave of sadness swept over her; there was a wistful look on her face. All she could mumble was, "It is taxing at this point."

Aseem took her hand and squeezed it, "We don't have to talk about it. We can however talk about dessert! Tiramisu, my lady?"

"Oh!... I'm not gonna share."

"Look at you, workout queen on a wild night out."

The evening flew by. He dropped her home and was a perfect gentleman. An evening like that was just what Naina needed; it removed her from her drab existence.

Aseem's visit to Delhi opened a new space in her heart. His going away almost made her feel sad and she couldn't wait to see him again. There were times when she felt guilty though about meeting another guy. Naina soon overcame that feeling when she realised that she was herself, sans any baggage, when around Aseem. Why didn't she feel the same vibes when she was with Rahul? Why did she feel a load on her shoulders when she was with Rahul? *Is this a clandestine affair that's brewing? Am I right to feel like 'myself' when I am with Aseem, and distant with Rahul? Is this cheating?*

Soon after Aseem's sudden appearance, the duo finalised their paragliding adventure trip to Dharamshala for a long weekend. They were part of a big group of other thrill seekers who were headed there. The people had met online through an adventure sports forum. Naina didn't give Rahul any reasons and asked for a leave. It was a refreshing break that made Aseem and Naina bond better as friends. However, each knew that the undercurrent of sexual attraction was growing strong between them. The weekend was over in a flash and soon after, life was back to a normal routine. Her outings with Aseem felt like a distant dream.

Naina's life took on a dramatic turn with Rahul. It had been a crazy hectic month and Naina had hardly spent any time with him.

Rahul was busy relocating a large French start-up. The entire relocation project was expected to take six months and entailed transferring employees, their families, and business departments to New Delhi.

After a busy day at work, they were together at Rahul's penthouse apartment in Gurgaon. Naina sunk into the chair and heaved a tired sigh.

"Hey Naina, do you want a glass of wine or a beer?"

She smiled at him, "Beer please."

Rahul decided to order in from the local Chinese restaurant because Ram Singh, his man Friday, was on leave for the day. None of them could be bothered with even tossing pasta. The food arrived rather quickly. They sat quietly. As Naina reached out for the noodles, Rahul casually said, "By the way, I am planning to take Mona to Kasauli to see the property during the week."

Naina stopped, a spoonful of noodles in her hand. She simply stared at Rahul, dumbstruck. He kept looking down at his plate and continued to eat as if he had shared a random, insignificant fact from a newspaper article with her. The sheer nonchalance pissed her off.

"You are taking 'my' associate from the office for a weekend to 'your' family home?" Naina said, her voice going from calm to 'hysterical' with every word. She could feel her face get hot with anger.

"*Uff*… Naina, can we just eat without arguing? I am tired and don't want to get into a conversation about this."

Naina stared at him in disbelief. "You casually drop a bomb and then don't want to talk about it?"

"It is not a bomb. And yes, that is exactly what I am saying," he said in a low grated tone.

Naina was completely shaken by the insensitivity of this man. She got up, in control, but deeply shocked. *This is a load of crap.* She stared down at him as he blankly looked up. "Fuck off, Rahul," saying so she walked out of the apartment.

She had never felt so angry before and a flux of emotions, ranging from despair, rage, and humiliation went through her. Hatred too. She hated herself at that moment. Her vulnerability post divorce and the thought of being alone made her cling to this relationship. *What a shameful weakness!*

It almost felt like déjà vu. She went down an unpleasant memory lane. Vikram, her ex-husband, had been physically abusive, a compulsive womaniser and a very demanding husband. Naina gave him 10 long years; she had been in an unhappy marriage for as far as she could recall.

It was easy to recount the exact moment that made her walk out of her marriage. It was the day Naina came home, unexpectedly, to find Vikram in bed with another woman. She had her suspicions all along about him being a womaniser, but to actually see it in her own bed was like being hit on the head with a hammer. Rather, it was the nail in the coffin for her marriage.

She remembered standing there for a second, in her head she wanted to bludgeon them to death. But all she did was ask the bimbette to leave and for him to come downstairs for a conversation. She didn't cry; she didn't throw a tantrum. Maybe she already knew in her heart it was happening. She had put up with Vikram's criticism and bullshit, but she thought he knew the line that was not to be crossed. She packed her bags and moved out never to return.

Naina wondered why life was so unpredictable, *No matter how hard I try and plan; it refuses to end up the way I want it to.*

Tara had always warned Naina, "Rahul is commitment phobic. It's got nothing to do with you, Naina. He just won't settle down…he's having too good a time for that." Naina wanted to prove Tara wrong. *But I can't. I can't do this again. It is like jumping from the frying pan into the fire. How could I let my life come to this? How could a man treat a woman like this? What the hell am I getting out of this relationship?*

Naina stepped out of the elevator and called for a cab. *That jackass is not going to come after me. Let him choke while he stuffs his face! Inconsiderate crackhead!*

Tears of anger rolled down her cheeks as she got into the cab. *I hate being used like this time and again...* Naina headed straight to Tara's house; she was inconsolable, angry and was losing control. What she needed at the moment was a shoulder to cry on. She wanted to surround herself with the comfort she knew Tara would give her. She entered Tara's house and broke down.

"I'm done with Rahul. It is over. Why doesn't life ever work out for me?"

Tara could see Naina in pain. The crazy thing was she knew that in the long run, it was the best thing for her to have walked out of the relationship. She hugged Naina and said, "Naina, stop blaming yourself. Stop treating yourself like an underdog in your own life. It is time to fix yourself first. Feel the love you are searching for within yourself, feel confident, and know that you are complete."

In a soft tone, almost as if she were consoling a child, Tara continued, "Take some time to reflect on the relationships in your life. Relationships act as mirrors; when we have a loving relationship with ourselves, the reflection will always be the strong, healthy one that we deserve. So look for that, Naina. Don't undermine yourself and sell yourself short. Things will work out for you...it's only a matter of time."

It had been a few days since the showdown at Rahul's apartment. Naina did her best to avoid Rahul at work. It was a blessing that their scope of work was different and their teams did not work directly with each other. It helped her to limit her interaction with him and she didn't need to engage in a conversation beyond work. He tried to strike up a conversation a few times, but she ignored him.

He doesn't think he has done anything wrong! He just comes up to have a chat? No apologies? No nothing! A week after his return from Kasauli, he called. He didn't apologise. He wanted to 'make plans' because he had time to kill. *I know the translation of that all too well, 'come on over, let's have sex'.* He called a few more times; she didn't answer and let it go to voicemail. He never left a message.

Finally, by that weekend, Naina was exhausted. It was time to come to terms with the inevitable end. She called Rahul and set up a 'we-need-to-talk' meeting. They met at her place that evening. He sat there fidgeting a little. He had a sheepish expression on his face. It was the look he got when he knew he was about to lose an argument, and in that moment, he became convincingly sincere. It was a true moment, but a fleeting one. She had experienced this before with him.

Naina sat on the stool across from him, leaned forward and clasped her hands. She was nervous, but ready. She took a deep breath and looked up at him, the realisation came to her, *He will never look beyond himself and that will always bring us back to the same place.* She sighed and ran her palm over her pencil skirt so as to smoothen out the creases on the fabric. *Let's do this.*

"Rahul, I don't know what you want in life, but I am pretty clear on what I want. And 'this' is not it. We've been together for two years. You are who you are; you will always be this guy. You don't know how to be true to anyone but yourself. That works for you. But it does not work for me. Not like this, not anymore."

She took a deep breath and continued in an even tone, "After my divorce, I am not looking to get stuck in a dubious relationship that is going to leave me lonely and isolated."

She looked at him with pain in her eyes, "You find ways to keep me on a leash. It's about whatever suits you. You are available to me, but not committed to me. I don't think you will ever be. I want a lot more. I deserve it! I have treated you well and been there for you as a companion... Look at you... you are barely here right now!"

She stopped, she didn't want to raise her voice, she didn't want an argument, she realised that she didn't want anything from Rahul anymore. "So please, just leave. Just finally go and don't look back this time." Her tone reflected the anguish inside her.

"Naina, don't do this." His demeanour was calm. He was not alien to this conversation. And he probably thought this was routine. But Naina was exhausted of living in this loop.

"No Rahul. It is time to call a spade a spade. I am sick of being there for you...with all I have and get a...half-hearted attempt in return. This was the last straw. It hurt...and you didn't think anything of it. How many times have you prioritised me over a night at the bar or a dinner? Is that what is supposed to happen in a relationship? I am not supposed to sit and wait for you while you find someone new to hit on for an evening of randomness. You don't want this relationship. If you did, you would know. You would prioritise me enough to give up playing games all the time. I don't have the energy to play the 20-year-old insecure girlfriend. I will not do it."

"I want happiness, even if it means being by myself, it is what I want most. I want wholeheartedness or nothing. And you... I am tired of dealing with your nonchalance and bullshit of a commitment. It is done, Rahul. We are officially done," Naina was on the verge of shouting, the pitch had gone up by some octaves. She tried hard to maintain her poise.

Rahul got up, walked across and sat on the stool next to her. Naina's eyes were glazed with tears. They were tears of anger, defeat and surrender. She had loved this man in a way that he would never understand…now, even she didn't. The fact that he didn't fight to remain in her life made her sad.

He took her hand, she let him. "You are right. I don't know how to give you what you want. I am not in a place where I want to settle down just yet…but you know, I can't see myself with anyone but you when I picture a swing on a porch and the retired life. You…we are so comfortable with each other."

Naina closed her eyes, a tear slid down her cheek and she whispered, "I can't wait for old age, Rahul… I want to live in the now. I can't wait for you to finish playing mystery bachelor to the world. I want dependability… I want companionship… I want someone to care…to care, 'now'. Not in some distant future."

"Naina…"

"No Rahul," she looked at him, "we can't go on like this… I can't. I can't watch you day in and day out mind-fucking me and leaving. You don't even know how much it affects me. You are just not aware. I am tired, Rahul. Don't you want me to be happy?" Tears were streaming down her face. She didn't care. "Please," she whispered, "let's stop."

Rahul sighed and looked at her. His eyes reflected her sadness. He lifted her hand up to his lips and kissed it gently. "I can't give you what you want, sweetheart. I am a bachelor at heart. But I want you to know that you will always be special to me. I will always love you. You made me happy."

Naina pulled her hand away, closed her eyes and let herself feel the pain of letting go of something that she really didn't want to give up. Her insides were screaming, *Please don't give up on us. Please.* But she kept quiet. She had gone from 'make me happy' to 'made me happy'. It was all 'past tense' now. He got up, kissed her on the head and slowly walked out the door. Naina sat there, broken. She knew she would never be the same again.

Since her break-up, Naina had been doing a lot of thinking and soul searching. December had been a very quiet holiday season for her this year. The question now for her was, *Where do I go from here? How do I figure out who I am and what I want? What is my new life going to look like, and how should I start moving in that direction?*

For starters, she wanted to distance herself from Rahul. She needed to filter her emotions and cut herself from all the baggage that she carried.

A lot had happened and Naina wanted to slow down her pace to what suited her. There was an empty space where someone once lived. And even though she didn't want him back in her life in that spot, she wanted to allow herself to grieve her loss, to mourn and to let the pain out of every screaming pore of her body.

Her divorce, her relationship with Rahul, it all came to her in a jiffy—probably, Rahul was a clone of Vikram. Why did she do this to herself…in loop? What was wrong with her—putting her career and kids on the backburner for a man who didn't even love or respect her? *How could I do this to myself?* Didn't she have even an iota of self-respect?

She was lying on the yoga mat in her bedroom as she whispered into the empty space, "I will gather the pieces and rebuild the mosaic of my life into something new. I will pick myself up, again." As she collected herself off the floor, she thought, *It's goodbye to everything I thought my life was and everything I thought it would be. Again. But this time, I will not repeat my mistakes. I can't handle going down this very path. Never again.*

As if on cue, she received a text message from Tara: We must be willing to get rid of the life we planned so as to have the life that is waiting for us.—Joseph Campbell

Naina smiled. It was comforting to know that even when she felt lonely, she was not alone. She knew her friend was grieving for her, with her. She also realised that whatever was happening in her relationships, they were definitely giving her an opportunity to grow stronger after every experience. She understood that growth meant learning from the past. Naina was aware that she had been in a pattern and wanted to break it.

The past six weeks had been an emotional roller coaster ride for Naina. Staying in touch with Aseem was reassuring and the devastation of feeling lonely was eased off.

It was not like she was invincible...she had her moments. One particular evening, Naina felt low. It was one of those days she knew she just needed to be calm and non-reactive and it would pass. She had read somewhere that writing how you felt was catharsis for the soul. She decided to write a letter to Rahul. Nothing that she would physically send out, but something that would set her free.

She wrote,

> I know what you feel like.
> I know what it is like to be your woman.
> I know how your magnetism works.

> I know what it is like to be drawn into those sincere looks you give… I know. Unfortunate…but I know all too well…
>
> It would be stupid to assume that you haven't already gotten over us. But I know you well enough to know I left some sort of impact on you. I have seen you in your element and I have seen you at your lowest point. I know that dark space you enter when you are alone; I have seen you through many such times. I am aware of how quickly that moment passes for you and you bounce back into your element.
>
> But I hope I changed you…as you changed me.
>
> I hope I am as bittersweet a memory for you as you are for me.
>
> I hope you look back and realise I was the one who got away.
>
> The person I am today would not have been if I hadn't experienced you. I am grateful for it and loathe it at the same time. I am aware that we have gone our separate ways and am happier for it. With time, this intensity will fade. It has already reduced. I am no longer hurt by you or attached to you. I pick up the phone and you are not the automatic call I make anymore. I see it in the small habits that are now breaking. They will soon be alien to me.
> Strangers, friends, lovers…and now back to strangers. We are the hackneyed break-up. But I am done to death with clichés.
>
> I am more aware than ever before that my life is about me.

Naina put the pen down. She felt much lighter. She resolved to herself that she wasn't going to over-extend herself for anyone anymore. To love and care the right amount is what she needed to be conscious of. She would do things that would make her happy.

Over the next few weeks, Naina got into a great routine of work and workouts. Aseem made Naina laugh; they spoke a lot more on the phone. They had gotten close over the past eight months. She spoke to him about Rahul, she did not go into the details but she mentioned the break-up. Over the course of the conversations, she became even more comfortable with him. *Maybe because he is still a close friend…*

She found a great deal of empathy from him, he was the man who had been with her since the beginning of the end. One day, over the phone, he said, "So, I won't hide that I am happy with the timing of the events. But, you want to talk about it?"

"I don't know Aseem…his lack of commitment just became too much for me to take. His flaunting other women under my nose and his constant philandering got to me. It is strange. I don't feel bitter or angry, but at the same time, I can't stop talking about it. I keep replaying our conversations or times spent."

"Look Naina, I don't know Rahul, I do know men though. And I can tell you right now that if a guy isn't up for a commitment, that relationship is not going anywhere."

"Yes, I realise that now. At the time, I thought I could make him change his mind."

"Classic mistake, woman! You can take a horse to the water, but you cannot make him drink."

"Oh thanks, Cliff! I feel a whole lot better now!" she smiled as she opened the fridge to get a cup of yogurt. "Okay, so you want to know what has changed for me? Up until recently, like many a misguided woman, I was looking for a man to complete me."

"God, no!"

"No no…it's unreal, but true. It is how I bought into the romantic notion." She sat on the kitchen counter and grabbed a spoon.

"But I hope you know better! It should actually be 'you complement me, not complete me.'"

"I know. It's funny you mention it because I have been thinking about it. That's the change I am bringing into my life." She popped open the yogurt and ate a spoonful.

"Exactly! Phew! And well, maybe it is time you start complementing yourself with the right ones…you know?"

She laughed, "That was very smoothly done! Subtle, aren't we?"

"Okay, okay…that was classic man of me."

Aseem made her smile. She liked the fact that she could speak out her mind in front of him.

Aseem told her that he was going to be in Delhi, the following weekend, for a few days. He asked Naina out for dinner. She hesitated. She was in this space of being by herself and for herself; she loved it and was in no mood to rush into anything at all.

She wanted to meet him, but she didn't think she was ready to get involved with anyone at this point. Naina was apprehensive about meeting Aseem. She wanted to give herself time. Her wounds were too raw at the moment.

"I don't know Aseem, maybe next time, okay?"

Aseem sighed, "Okay, no worries. Next time. I don't want to push you."

Overlooking the fireplace in her cosy sitting area, her mind wandered. *What a guy! He respects my space and is patient. For him, I am my own individual. I count. Wow…that feels weird. Rahul always needed it his way. Am I used to being treated like I don't count?*

Aseem came to Delhi the following weekend and called up Naina. She was just back from work.

"Hello! So you are in town?"

"Yes. But there's no one to show me around… Nothing in this city is 'tempting' enough."

Naina laughed, "Oh really! I thought 'work' was tempting enough."

"C'mon Temptress! You know what I mean. But then, I am tied up with meetings and presentations till day after, and then I do have a day to please myself in your city."

"I will see how I can make your free day more pleasurable, my friend," said Naina, in a mock formal tone.

After the conversation, Naina got thinking, *Why don't I meet up with Cliffhanger again? Am I scared of something…that I am resisting meeting him? I deserve a chance with happiness. Not as a rebound space but as a fresh start. This one's for me. I will take it slow, one day at a time, at my pace. I don't have to rush into calling it a relationship. Heck, I don't owe Cliff any explanation at this point. We are on an even, equal ground. It is just a friendly dinner.*

She sent Aseem a message, "I would be honoured to accompany you day after to paint the town red!"

Her phone pinged after a few minutes, "Great! I look forward to it. Cliff."

They planned to meet up for dinner. The crisp January winter evening was perfect for an outdoor drink. They decided to meet at the deck of the hotel where Aseem was staying and then grab dinner at the Japanese restaurant there.

Naina was looking forward to the evening. She dressed up in her favourite blue shift top, slim jeans and ankle-length brown boots and leather jacket. She put her phone, cards, and keys in her messenger leather bag. She mentally ticked off the hair-do and light make-up; both looked just right. A quick squirt of her signature light 'jasmine' fragrance and she was on her way to meet Aseem.

As she walked towards the deck, Naina was suddenly aware of the fact that this got real in her single space. She walked in, took a deep breath and looked around. At the far end of the bar, he stood tall. He was looking directly at her with a crooked smile. The one that seemed to say, *Let the fun begin.*

Naina walked towards him, smiling. She felt confident and the warmth and naughtiness in his smile calmed her. He was wearing a grey cashmere with a pair of dark blue jeans and brown formal shoes. *Casual and cool,* she thought, *I like it.*

It had been a while since she met Aseem and she had forgotten how dapper he looked. Naina had a flash of Rahul in her head; he was as tall as Aseem, maybe broader but as fit. They shared the same fair complexion. Naina subconsciously rated them, against each other, on looks. *Rahul: 9.5, Cliffhanger: 7.89. Stop it; you aren't some 10/10 bombshell! And you are not with Rahul anymore anyway.*

Aseem escorted her to a stool at the bar. She sat and looked at him with a smile, "So, is this place good enough for you? Or it doesn't quite meet your Mumbai standards?"

He laughed, "It's a cool place, thanks for recommending it."

"So, how was business?"

"Good. I just came in time to quickly change and head downstairs."

"Perfect."

"What would you like to drink, love? Your usual? Vodka, soda with a twist of lime?"

"Oh, so have been paying attention. Yes, please. How about you? A glass of red wine? A Cabernet, right?"

"Not bad, not bad. So far we both are doing well."

They laughed. There was no denying the spark between them; it was almost tangible. It was not just a conversation connect, she was attracted to him and she couldn't discount it. She felt like a heady teen on a first date. It was a nice feeling.

Aseem was sensitive and witty. It was refreshing for Naina that he didn't suffer the typical 'me-man syndrome'. He was curious about her; when he spoke to her, he looked at her as if she was the only person on earth. He wanted to know more about her life. He was confident and they touched on a lot of varied topics. They shared their views on politics, to her 'secret' love for chocolate.

He laughed, "How come you didn't tell me about this 'secret' love of yours before? But wait, you have a secret stash of chocolate that you hide from yourself? How is that a secret? You know where you hid it!"

"Oh shush!...I know it sounds absurd. But it works, okay!"

He laughed and shook his head as he picked up his glass. He took a sip of his wine while looking at her, his eyes reflecting his amusement. She felt a little self conscious, so she too sipped on her drink.

They talked about their respective jobs, current statuses and their professional growth. Naina wanted to eventually start her own firm. Aseem was working to become a senior partner and a board member at his firm.

"I like the 'environment' I work in," he said, while he made air-quote gestures with his hands. "Pun intended," he smiled. "How do you see yourself heading the business?"

"Well, with my ex-husband, I used to work in his family business. Managing people and playing the leadership role comes naturally to me."

He looked at her, "Sexy-entrepreneur-business-lady... I like it."

She smiled. He didn't probe into her marriage or the lack of it. He was so easy to spend time with, she was glad she came for dinner.

The conversation did mention Rahul. She told Aseem how she felt she was working too hard to save something that didn't exist.

"I am sorry. I shouldn't be sharing this with you. It is girlfriend talk!"

"No no no...please. I love to hear all about the ex-boyfriend of a woman who intrigues me."

"Ha ha...I intrigue you?"

"There is a certain genuineness about you, Naina. It is rare. You are strong, yet gentle...personally, that is how a woman should be. And that, sweetheart, is intriguing."

Naina looked at him, rolled her eyes, and laughed, "Do women really fall for that stuff?"

"Okay, it sounds cheesy. But it is true. The façade behind the Temptress 007 came crumbling through in the first chat. Now, tell me something, why did a fine woman like you go for a douchebag? Can we please agree to leave that behind and change direction?"

Naina looked at him.

"I don't know. But try convincing me that things will be better off with you and I'll take it into consideration," she flirted back.

The flirtatious banter was spontaneous and electric; it continued all evening. The ambience in the restaurant was a nice intimate one and the duo shared excellent sashimi as they chatted. The setting was perfect.

He makes me feel like everything is going to be all right. It is nice to put Rahul in the 'over-and-done-with' rack at the back of my mind…

They slowly walked out into a busy lobby. Naina relaxed in his company and felt secure in her own skin.

"By the way, how did you get here?"

"Oh! A private taxi. I like to use that service at night. Just safer, you know."

"Well, in that case, I shall drop you home. I have arranged for a car during my stay here."

"No, no. There is no need. You must be tired. It's quite far and…"

Aseem cut her off, "Jeez, I didn't get off some 20-hour flight and had back-to-back meetings. I offered because I want to. It will just give me some more time with you. Is that a problem?" He had a twinkle in his eyes.

Naina looked up at his face, the warmth in his eyes made her smile. *How sincere. Such a simple thing made me feel so special.* "I'd like that," she said.

It was a quiet ride. She got a little nervous. Aseem looked over at her and smiled.

"Would you like to come up for a coffee?" She laughed nervously. "Yes, yes, I know 'coffee' is the code for 'sex', but the truth is, I don't want this evening to end. Not just yet."

He had a big hearty laugh, "All right woman, coffee it is."

They stood in the kitchen while she brewed the coffee—an Arabica blend that she loved. "Black with one spoon of sugar, right?"

"Yes, same as you."

They smiled. They sure as hell knew a lot about each other with all the chatting. She relaxed; *I guess these chats opened a whole new way to get to know each other because the conversations can be so simple and random.*

They headed to the two-seater couch.

"Nice place."

"Thanks."

"So, Naina, what is it that I don't know about you yet?"

"What do you mean?"

"Well, okay. What is the strangest pick-up line ever used on you?"

"Ha ha!... Seriously? That would have to be yours, today! Ha ha!"

He put his mug down on the coffee table and looked at her. "If you didn't intrigue me, I would not be here right now. See, men will be men. I'd rather be straightforward with you. So yes, you intrigue me; I would like to get to know you better. And Naina, I would rather be here than anywhere else."

She quickly got up from her seat and changed the topic, "Strangest pick-up line?"

He laughed. "Oh no! You don't get to throw my question back at me."

He picked up his coffee, walked over and stood next to her. He put his arm around her lower back and slowly turned her towards him. He looked at her. There was a soft, gentle look about him. "Naina, I know you have been through a lot. I understand your apprehensions. I know, even now, you have a lot going on in this head of yours. But I have to tell you that I had an amazing evening. We have this… this chemistry, but I want to give this time. I don't want to end up being the buffer—an emotional cushion that lessens the impact of your break-up. You need some breathing time, you deserve someone different…but only when you are ready. I am right here."

He bent down and kissed her lightly on the lips. It was like he wanted to seal what he had said. He stepped back and his usual charming robust self was back as he said, "But for now, I am going to leave."

He walked towards the door, "Ciao bella. Thanks for the coffee." He looked back at her flushed face, "Try not to stay up thinking about me!" The red on her cheeks deepened. She smiled as she thought, *Cliffhanger…Aseem. This is better than I expected.*

6

Therapy Session

Neil had been giving Tara a tough time; he was skipping classes and missing project deadlines. Tara was making sure that she spent as much time as possible with him. She tried her best to talk to him like a friend rather than a parent. It worked, but not for long. It was a delicate situation. She didn't want him to become averse to her parenting and withdraw from her. She wanted to create the right home environment for Neil to grow into a more responsible individual. But he was beginning to test her patience to the extreme.

On the work front, Tara had been busy with a new hotel that was opening soon and she was up to her neck with deadlines. She felt the need to focus on her son and work.

Tara did her best to keep herself preoccupied. Tara reached out to Goo-gle in her quiet time. Talking on the phone had helped them grow a lot closer.

In a way, Nihal and her story ran at parallels. They were both at crossroads trying to wade through life. She was looking forward to meeting Nihal at the Gymkhana Club. After weeks of persuasion, he had finally conceded to meet Naina and her.

Nihal was a regular guy, from a decent family, and whatever little doubts about safety that she had had about meeting him, was washed away as she got to know him better with each conversation that they had. He was now her friend. Naina was very keen to meet him as well. Tara had confirmed if Nihal was comfortable meeting both of them.

While driving, she realised how important Nihal had become to her. In Nihal she found a confidante, someone on whom she could offload her heart without fear. It was different than having a girlfriend, Nihal was far more empathetic. He was a gentle, kind-hearted person. Tara compared Nihal's confusing situation and her's and found herself re-questioning her life. She now wanted a solution and didn't want to settle for anything less. She relived the chat she had had with Nihal about her mess.

(10:16 pm) Ubercool: nowadays, all I can think of is having an affair with Nutty

(10:16 pm) Goo-gle: maybe, he's the spice or the unpredictability that you are looking for in your relationship…

(10:17 pm) Ubercool: ya, for sure, considering the husband situation

(10:17 pm) Goo-gle: it can become a little bit of drag… if it's been long.

(10:17 pm) Goo-gle: You have not been with anyone apart from your husband?

(10:17 pm) Goo-gle: after marriage?

(10:18 pm) Ubercool: never, no… boring… really deserve to now… before I become old

(10:18 pm) Goo-gle: hmm… I understand

(10:18 pm) Ubercool: So, is it wrong? To think like this… I'm married… a mother… so what! what's wrong with me?

(10:19 pm) Goo-gle: no... not really... sweetheart ... Morally, it maybe wrong... bt you have all the right to live for yourself

(10:19 pm) Ubercool: Thanks :)

(10:20 pm) Ubercool: Yes! But I don't have a right to cheat... I find that morally wrong. Is it possible to be in love with both men? I am losing my mind here. I feel like I can't make a choice because I love them both. I am scared to lose my husband. Scared of making the wrong choices. Oh! I am just tired Goo-gle. I don't want to hurt anybody and I don't want to hurt myself

She entered the Gymkhana and pulled up in the parking. *A spot! That was quick.* She parked and headed for the coffee shop. She was running a bit late and wondered if Nihal and Naina had already reached or would they keep her waiting. She hated it when people came late for meetings and kept her hanging. She entered the coffee shop and looked around for Nihal. Suddenly she heard her name from across the tables, "Tara!"

She looked around and saw a young man in jeans and a crème T-shirt standing in front of the lawn entry. Completely clean shaven with short hair, Nihal stood in front of her as a man. She was flummoxed; she was so used to imagining Nihal as Niharika.

Naina walked in just behind Tara. "Hi, perfect timing!" They walked towards Nihal. Hugs exchanged, they grabbed a table.

This image of Nihal as a man completely threw Tara offguard, "For the first time it hit me that you are a man, not a woman!" They all laughed. Once she got used to the idea that Niharika was Nihal first, that he was a man, they all got along like a house on fire.

The three of them chatted non-stop. A designer with one of the top retailers in Delhi, Nihal was also a photographer. They shared common passions—design, theatre, music and art.

"You two are so lucky to be born as women! Don't take it for granted. Why don't you take more interest in yourself?" Tara was taken aback by the bluntness, but smiled because she knew this was innocence. Nihal was far from rude, he was just very very simple and naïve.

"Why do you ladies dress up so plain and classic? Spend some time over how you look. Use your face as a canvas and enhance your looks. Explore different strokes, colours…see what suits you best."

Naina laughed, "Ha ha! Gosh! You are such a girl! I seriously feel a lesser woman with you right now."

Nihal was very endearing; he had a certain vulnerability about him that made both the women feel protective towards him. "Coffee, guys? Waiter!" Tara called out.

Both Tara and Naina could see that Nihal was at the edge of a precipice, and that it was tough for him to keep up the charade. It was only a matter of time before his whole being would come tumbling down.

Once the waiter left with their order, Nihal leaned forward, "One second ladies, I have something important to share." Nihal told them that he recently went to a therapist because he wanted to end this life of duplicity.

Tara encouraged, "I am so happy that you are finally ready to take responsibility. Why? Your desire to become a woman in all aspects has finally found expression. Think about it Nihal, it means you are ready."

Nihal confessed to her that he was tired of hiding beneath a mask for years. "I have been brought up in a normal, happy, upper-middle class family environment. My dad is an IAS officer and my mum is a homemaker. I have a sister. We are a regular family; my parents instilled the usual values which every middle-class parent would instill in their child. When I hit puberty, I began to realise who I really was. But I lived in fear that if anyone ever saw the real me, it would destroy our perfect family. I tried my best to suppress my feelings, hoping they would just go away. But I refused to confide my deep dark secret with them."

"It can't have been an easy journey, sweetheart! That is why I am so keen that you change it. Get a better life," Tara begged him.

"You know, life is not easy for transgenders in India. They hide their identity for fear of rejection; uncertain whether it is right to feel the way they feel and want what everyone around them finds wrong. Most transgenders are ill treated and harassed by the public. My own recent crazy date is proof enough! I don't have the guts to come clean yet. It would kill my parents and I don't want them to be the butt of ridicule in their narrow-minded society. And so the show must go on... Their son! What a joke! No matter how hard I try, I can't be their son. I couldn't be a brother or a boy. That's just not who I am. It is not who I really am. I am a failure..."

Naina cut him off, "You are looking at it all wrong, Nihal. Not being a 'son' doesn't make you a bad child or a terrible sibling. From what I heard, you seem to have a great relationship with your sister. Your sexual orientation doesn't matter in these relationships. Your family will always love you. Unconditionally."

Tara's heart broke when she heard Nihal talk. "God is so complete in his vision. Nothing that is done is a mistake. I watched a play recently, 'The Third Gender' by Peter Zachary. The concept brought me to realise that transgenders were god's way of finding the middle path, to find balance, to converge the Yin and the Yang."

Nihal looked down at his coffee, "Maybe you are right. I want to believe it is that simple and easy to accept."

Naina moved in closer, "Now listen to me and trust me on this one. I am sure if you tell your parents and come clean you will be a much happier person. And they will be happy to see you happy."

A startled look flashed across Nihal's face, "Temptress, I have painted the scenario in my head over a billion times. Not a single situation that I have imagined ends on a happy note. My parents are super conservative and homophobic! So what should I tell them? Hi! I'm 26, I am a man on the outside but a girl on the inside! I cross-dress and I want to be screwed by a man."

Naina smiled, "You tell them exactly that. Except leave the 'screwed by a man' part out. They don't need such explicit details." The waiter arrived with the coffee and served the three of them.

"Sugar?"

"Yes please, one spoon." The waiter left them to get on with their conversation.

Nihal took a sip of his coffee and sighed, "No! Their world would crumble thinking they have not known their child at all. Ever! They would be ashamed in their precious 'society'. Come on, I can't be this insensitive."

"It is a matter of time, Nihal." Tara added, "One day or the other, it is inevitable that your family will know. Have faith in your love for your folks. Parents come around, all the time. Anything goes for your own kids. You are not being insensitive."

Nihal looked dazed. Tara continued to convince him. "Remember, you once told me that I have a right to be happy? You owe the same to yourself; have the courage to stand by your convictions. This one's for you. If you are so sure that you want to be a woman, go ahead and be one! You have a right to live for yourself and to give happiness a chance!"

"And," Naina added, "your family will be supportive because you won't be living in deception. This dual life is very hard and absolutely not worth it. It is not an easy way. Unfortunately, you will take time to adjust and you might have reactions that are unfair, but look past that. They will accept who you are because the person inside you, man or woman, is a beautiful, kind-hearted individual." She sipped her coffee, and continued, "I mean, look at you…you are so considerate, you are ready to live like this for the sake of your parents! They should be proud that they brought you up well in this world of millennials."

"Exactly!" Tara encouraged.

"I know!" Tara squealed with excitement as she got an idea, "You could take a break and go to Thailand. There are so many transgenders there; you would get a chance to explore the possibility of a sex-change operation. Go meet a doctor. Why don't you go, just for the heck of it? Tell your parents you need a break and make that trip your survey.

The road to your final destination is fraught with many a pitfall. But it's a road that's being traversed more frequently now. Why don't you take a chance and explore? Being in the thick of it, you will be convinced about how right it is for you."

Nihal looked a bit pensive and replied, "I know who I am, Ubercool. For sure. But you are right; doing a recce won't hurt anyone. I have leaves to spare. And I have often thought about it, but, didn't think about planning it." And then he snapped into reality, "Oh! But I can't imagine how my parents would react!" Nihal was getting upset.

"Okay…okay… Let's not go there yet." Naina calmed him down, "Small steps first. Why not just go to Thailand and check it all out first. Then, you can come back and reassess how you will go about it. And you can think about telling your parents then. What say?"

On a lighter vein into the conversation, Naina continued, "Look at all the fun that you would have! Bad girls have fun in Thailand; good girls go to heaven."

Nihal finally cracked up for the first time that evening, "You're a naughty bitch…aren't you? Ha ha!…I so want to be someone's girl. I mean it…but that someone has to be a little decent."

Tara winked, "Ya ya…go have some fun."

"Yes, okay…I promise to think about it. For now that is all. I need to do that before I go under the knife anyway. I think if I have to do my research in Thailand, having this test done will show them I am serious about going under the knife for my peace of mind! But that is for later… For now, Tara, don't eat my head up. I 'will' think about all this. Okay?"

Tara laughed. He knew him well. She would get on his case. "Good. Yes, transitioning is a very serious step in life and you really shouldn't rush into anything. It could take a few sessions with a psychologist to make a confirmed diagnosis and from there, they can continue working with you through the transitioning process."

Nihal looked at Tara in amazement. "What? Ya ya! I've been reading a lot on the Internet. There is a support group that exists in Delhi, you could even join it."

Nihal rolled his eyes and laughed, "*Uff*, enough for now. Too many ideas rolling around your head! Ha ha ha..."

They finished their coffees over laughs on silly *Cupidity* chats they had had and how ridiculous people sounded sometimes over the chat site. In this regard, the mention of Pepper & Salt could not be avoided! That guy was a winner if they were competing with online stories. An hour later, the three parted on a note of, "Great balls of fire! After all, tomorrow is another day!"

7

Live Wire, Exposed

It was late on a Saturday night. Tara paced up and down the living room in her kaftan. Neil was not home yet. It was quite unlike him. It was close to midnight. *Where is this boy? He should have been home by 10!* That was his curfew time. She called him yet again. No answer. *Dammit Neil!* Where the hell was he? She must've called him close to 50 times now. She wanted to redial non-stop, but controlled herself and called with time gaps. She didn't want to be a freak. *I am sure he is playing video games at one of the boy's houses and has his phone on silent. That's got to be it.*

Neil was a regular kid. He was easy to handle, but he needed to be a little more focussed at this stage in his life. Tara felt that he had the brains but lacked the ambition. She would have liked had Ranvir stepped in and moulded the boy into a man. Neil had reached a stage where he needed a mentor, and who better than his father to assume that role. Unfortunately, he was hardly there. These were crucial years and the next few were a big leap in his life. Tara wanted him to be geared to take life head on.

She called Ranvir, not sure what else to do. He was mad about it, "Why are you calling me? Why the hell did you let him go in the first place? I will try calling him right now."

"What the hell will that do?"

"I don't know…what else can I do from here?" He hung up on her.

Tara changed into a pair of track pants and a sweatshirt. *I am going to go over to every friend's house in the colony till I find him and I will pull him by the ears and bring him home!*

"Oh god, let him be at his friend's place!" she whispered as she got into the car. Neil was a good kid. Sure, he had the general naughty streak in him like all kids do, like pulling a girl's leg, playing a prank on a teacher; the healthy, fun stuff. But he wasn't notorious. He didn't get into trouble or have a notorious reputation. On the contrary, Tara was pretty proud of Neil, not only as a son, but also as a student, friend, and athlete. *No credit to Ranvir. That asshole has not been around our son in the most important years of development. This adolescence phase is when fathers and sons bond. This guy has been away throughout.* And now, as she sped through the colony, she was cursing Ranvir for being an absent father while her son went missing!

All of a sudden, the car screeched to a halt. In the darkness, in the play of the irregularly lit street lamp, she saw a shadow stumbling on the path in her direction. "Neil!" she yelled as she got off the car. She was angry and relieved at the same moment. *Drunk! Alive!*

This was a first. Neil was so focussed on his swimming track team. He represented his school at the state level. There was no room to get involved in any rubbish when the pressure to perform was so intense. She could not figure out how this happened. She ran towards him. He looked up, eyes bloodshot, "Mom!" a shocked look and then a laugh. "Mom, mommy, mom, mom! What are you doing here?"

he giggled. Hic! Tara's anger knew no bounds and it took all her self-control to keep herself from smacking him hard across the face. "What are you doing here?" she asked in a grated low tone.

He stumbled. Tara helped him up and staggered with his body weight on her side as she swung his heavy arm across her shoulder. "I was at Ashish's house and we played some video games. Shh!… We are not allowed there, in the basement, but even his dad is not there." He said as she led him to the car. "These dads and their 'business travels,'" he slurred, air-quoting the last two words, as he slid in the backseat. "I just feel so woozy. I want to sleep."

Tara got in the driver's seat and drove home. She was in a rage, but at the same time, was very concerned about what he drank, how much, and a zillion other questions. At that very moment, she was focussed. She had to take care of this kid right now. *Man, I don't know what fucking crazy things we can endure when it comes to our kids. We just can.*

Her phone rang, "Ya! I got him Ranvir. He is with me; I am on my way home. He is drunk. Let me handle him. I will call you later."

Tara took Neil into the house. Over the next 45 minutes, she ran around from his loo to the room, to the kitchen—water, lime juice, vomit, cleaning, vomit again. Neil was totally incoherent. He kept apologising, and much as she wanted to hit him, she kept her anger in check and helped him into bed.

Finally, he passed out. She placed a waste paper bin next to him and a bottle of water on his bedside.

She sunk into the couch. *I am a mess. How the hell did this happen to my kid? Why? I know at this age they are curious, but*

Neil knows better. He is responsible. What the hell was this out of the blue outburst of drinking?

It was not that drinking scared her. Tara had brought up her son in a home where a pre-dinner beer, whisky or wine was not an alien concept. Both mother and son knew that someday he would sit with his family and chat over a drink. But that someday was definitely not now. It definitely was not to sneak into a friend's dad's basement bar and drink silly and then try and walk back home in the middle of the night. *What the hell was going on?*

She picked up the phone and pressed '2' on her Speed Dial. Exhausted from all the tension, and frustrated about her son, she called her husband.

"You know Ranvir, I've had it! I can't handle Neil any longer; I don't know how to handle him. He's a teenager with raging hormones and he needs a dad by his side at this stage. You are too busy absconding—the stay-away husband, the stay-away father. Why the fuck did you get married if you wanted to abandon us and run the fuck off? I am not here to raise this boy on my own!" She was shaking with anger and it was clear in her tone.

Ranvir tried to get a word in throughout but Tara wouldn't let him. He said that Neil was just a teenager and experimenting with things, it was natural. She didn't want to hear it. She went on.

"For the sake of your kid, come back. You are a selfish MCP! You only think of yourself; you have never thought about me? And Neil? Does he mean nothing to you? I took a back seat in my career just to support you, but you couldn't care less. I hate you and regret the day I married you! I have got nothing but pain from this marriage. I have all the responsibilities, while you are busy self-actualising and gallivanting away. Why don't you understand that it is tough for me to handle everything here all by myself! Why don't you look for an assignment in Delhi? It is important you be here. You will regret it one day. It's a matter of two years; then Neil goes to college. Isn't our son important to you? I have decided, if you don't get back, I'm quitting—that's it!"

He said he would speak to Neil when he woke up, but Tara was so upset that she banged the phone on him and resolved to pack her bags and call it quits. She was seething and had had it with Ranvir.

Tara felt that it was a different matter altogether to be a negligent father and could never forgive Ranvir for not being with her to raise their son. Ranvir tried calling a couple of times, but she was so angry that she cut the line every time.

She took out the suitcase from under the bed, threw open her cupboard and started to dump clothes into the suitcase. Tara caught a glimpse of herself in a mirror—tears streaming down her face, she looked sad and defeated. She stopped and sat on the bed. Still. Tara was in such a dilemma, hurt because she felt alone and abandoned.

She lay down, exhausted and broken. *My husband is no longer my friend. He is never there for me when I need him the most. He lives his life as if we weren't married. We're like ships passing in the night—he goes his way and I go mine. How the hell will Neil and I go on like this? This is just the beginning of his change.* She cried into the pillow as her thoughts took over her existence.

She messaged Nutty, "My husband has become a stranger to me. I don't even know who he is anymore. He doesn't show any interest in me or what I do." It was late so she didn't expect a response, but she reached out to him nonetheless. He was her 'safe' space. But tonight, she felt all alone. Nutty couldn't help her even if he were present now and even if he tried.

The tears kept coming; she had not cried this much in a long time. She couldn't believe this could be happening to her. She tried to stop it but just couldn't. She was so upset about Neil that she finally broke into sobs. She had no fight left in her. She thought she could keep this inside her, all bottled up. She thought if she put it in the back of her mind, it would go away in due time. She was wrong, keeping all these emotions inside just got too much to endure and now here she was, defenceless. *Tonight... Tonight I'll cry. I'm going to let everything out, everything I've been keeping deep inside me.*

8

At the Crossroads

Tara was still angry with Ranvir after the Neil incident. She felt she had put in a lot of herself in the marriage and didn't want to be taken for granted. It was not okay for her to spend her life waiting for her husband. *The men have no idea what it takes to make a woman happy! Take responsibility, man!*

At this point, Tara was in a dilemma like never before. She felt she was torn into two; a part of her still felt committed to Ranvir. She remembered the early days of her marriage when Neil was a baby and Ranvir was attentive to her every need. She had felt nurtured and life had a purpose. That always gave her hope that things would work out with Ranvir. She wanted her marriage to work, to feel like a complete unit. However, as Neil became a bigger part of her life, Ranvir became totally consumed by his work life—there was nothing left for her. She, on the other hand, was totally committed to her family and gave it her all. But she knew, in her heart, that she wanted more out of her life.

She went back to a conversation with Ranvir, close to four years ago. It was around the time he had started travelling a lot for work. They spoke about how important it was to nurture each other in a relationship, to grow in a relationship, to have common interests and to drive the marriage to the next level.

"Look Tara, you know I love you, right?" They were sitting in the living room over a nightcap—Brandy, their favourite tradition.

"I love you too, Ranvir. But 'love' is a strange term that has many connotations and translates into various forms as life goes on. We both entered this marriage out of choice with a will to make it work. It was the cornerstone of our lives; by each other's side forever, as it should be. But I don't feel you are in the marriage anymore. You are so emotionally distant it makes me wonder if we even have a connect!"

"I am here… I am doing this for us as a family…"

"No, you took on these projects to get away."

"Tara, that is not true." He got up and refilled his glass. "I am going where there is work."

"Sweetheart, I know you well enough. Convince yourself, not me, you don't 'need' to do this for us, you need it to challenge yourself as a professional. And I am ok with that."

"Then what do you want?" He said in an irritated tone as he turned to face her.

"I don't know, Ranvir… I feel like we're a million miles apart. I don't like living in isolation—you leaving Neil and me. But I haven't stopped you. So support me in my desires too!" She gulped her last sip in frustrated anger. *This is not how we used to drink brandy, never was it such a hostile environment.*

"I do support you—interiors, art and whatever else."

"I don't mean work, Ranvir, I mean in life. I want you to participate in my life from time to time." She put the glass down, "I don't want to feel emotionally abandoned by you. I want to feel a part of a unit, to feel connected. How did our marriage reach this point? Let's trace it back to the times we did things together. Things we loved that made us feel alive, feel together."

"Ok, let's do this. Every time I come back, we will do something exclusive at least twice a week. Once, anything you like, and the other something I like... Now, does that work?"

"Ya... see? That wasn't so hard, was it?"

But the problem came when Ranvir's words didn't translate into action. His time at work always exceeded the time spent at home, and their marriage gradually trickled down to a mere bite together at dinner or a brief chat on the phone. A good marriage required face-to-face time, both talk and fun. She just felt stonewalled by him.

Tara had worked on her marriage. *God knows I tried!* She remembered the time she visited Ranvir in Singapore while he was on an assignment. He was so busy, he would join her for a late dinner and nothing more. Even on weekends, he was buried in paperwork and coordinations with his base in India. Tara felt left out and inconsequential. That was even lonelier than being in her routine in Delhi.

Over the years, he had stopped investing in the marriage, leaving her feeling detached and unwanted. To the outside world the situation still looked rosy, but in reality, the relationship was dying a slow, quiet death. Years of feeling uncared for made it easier for her to drift apart. They weren't a couple with fierce conflict; they were just a couple who had different ideas of 'love' and 'companionship'. She felt she was hanging onto this marriage with one foot in and one out. For her, this marriage had hit an all-time low.

Still upset, Tara met up with Nutty for a coffee. The weather was changing, March had brought in an early heat wave. "Cold coffee please," Tara ordered, distractedly. Nutty was aware of the disquiet in her mind, "What's going on, Tara? I can sense you are all over the place in your head."

"Yes, I am. I don't know. Sometimes I feel like just ending this charade of a marriage. I'm so confused. Anyway, I don't want to drag you into it."

"Umm… I am already into it by default. So here I go again, what is going on, Tara?"

Tara laughed, "Nutty, the emotional route into a woman's pants? Nice!"

"Hey, it works!"

"You know, sometimes life seems like a mess. Then when you look at others, you thank god for being normal for the life that you have."

"What are we talking about?"

"I was on *Cupidity* some time back and I got chatting with this person…Goo-gle. Well, actually he is a man but wants to be a woman."

"Hey! A moment to express how deeply wounded I feel! Woman, you have an appetite—despite the two men in your life, you still feel the need for *Cupidity*?"

Tara laughed and rolled her eyes, "Nutty, this guy is a transgender. He is a woman trapped in a man's body. He is in his 20s. You know how hard that could be to live with?"

"I am not a homophobe...but I am happy to admit, I have no idea what that must feel like. I am a simple man who loves to enter a woman's body."

"Ha ha! You gigolo!"

"Come on! Below the belt, I mean below the belt...with you."

"You are incorrigible," she jokingly slapped his hand.

"Anyway," Tara emphatically changed the topic. "He is such a sweetheart and Naina and I video chatted with him when he dressed up like a woman. And Nutty, he was gorgeous!" She decided to refrain from getting into his recent abusive date. She respected him enough to not make it part of a light coffee conversation.

"This gender change is confusing me. But I would be happy to do the two of you together. The dauntless valiant is at your service forever."

"I'm serious, Nutty."

"Okay, so... What...are you thinking? What has that got to do with you?"

"Well, I want to help him a bit. Currently, he is afraid to come clean in front of his own family and friends. He needs to realise that his life is his own and to transition to his chosen identity will probably give him a sense of clarity, of peace. He is so troubled living two completely different lives, the poor soul. Just imagine the kind of anguish he must face of not being true to himself. What a huge burden to carry around. He wants to go to Thailand; apparently, it is the best and safest place for a sex-change operation, but he can't make up his mind. Basically, he doesn't have the courage. I want to support him a bit, you know, hold his hand..."

Nutty was smiling; there was affection in his eyes.

Tara stopped rambling and looked at him, "What?"

"Be the friend you want to be to this guy or girl. But don't get yourself into any trouble. I really love that crazy compassion you have, please be careful though. You don't know what's going on in his head."

Tara didn't need Nutty's seal of approval, but she was thrilled that she got it so easily. He took her hand and lifted it to his lips and gently kissed it. Tara blushed and laughed like a silly teenager.

A few days later, she was in the kitchen making pizza for Neil. She read the caller id. It was Ranvir. She picked up the phone.

"What? I'm busy." She was stonewalling him now.

"Hey! I know how upset you are with me. I'm really sorry about not being with you when you needed me the most."

She was quiet. He grabbed the opportunity to continue, "Tara, I'm really sorry that you are so upset. I've been thinking about us as a family, and I think you are right about Neil and you needing me. I'm coming back for a fortnight next month to Delhi."

"What about your work?" She asked in a dry tone, while she thought, *I don't really care about your work anymore. And I don't really believe you are willingly coming home.*

"I am going to try and explore some work possibilities in Delhi." He sounded like he expected her reaction. He knew it wasn't an option to commit and go back on his word anymore. Dangerous ground. *Finally! He really thought this through… Whatever!*

"Whatever, Ranvir! At this point, I don't know what to believe with you. You are here today, gone tomorrow. I don't even know… I just feel used. I get to look after the house and grate, while the master simply checks out."

Ranvir cut her off, "I know, I know… I think we are losing touch with each other and we need to work things out. I know my taking these offshore assignments has been very tough on you. Let's see how to work things between us, okay? I still love you."

Tara had a series of overwhelmingly strong emotions that were contradictory. For the sake of Neil, she was happy to have Ranvir back. But on the other hand, she was panicking at the thought of losing Nutty. She loved Ranvir in a very distant kind of way, now, but she had developed strong feelings for Nutty. She wondered if it was possible to be polyamorous.

In a state of panic, she called up Naina and updated her on Ranvir's return to Delhi. "Now that Ranvir is headed back, why do I fear his return? What do I do? I obviously can't tell Ranvir about Nutty. How will I meet Nutty when Ranvir is back?"

Naina calmed her down, "Tara, you can't have your cake and eat it too. If you want your marriage to work, I say go for it. Give your marriage a last chance. Do whatever you have to do to make it work—light candles, buy sexy lingerie, stop being the nag, go out as a family and as a couple, try talking to each other, explain yourself to him, reconnect… But please be patient with him. And then if you still feel that matters aren't improving, well, then think about it. For now, you better stop meeting Nutty because it would seriously cloud your judgement. One step at a time, love."

"And is it not unfair to Nutty?"

"Ya, that too," Naina laughed. "Hey! Maybe I sould take over Nutty from you. More the merrier, right?"

"Ha ha... You moron! Enjoy the one guy. Trying to be the alter ego in your real existence, are you? Tsk tsk... What have I created?" Tara felt better. *One step at a time, love.*

"You know what? I am going to lead parallel lives. So much for not knowing how Nihal leads dual lives! In my own context, I get it now! Okay, I love Ranvir, but he has to work really hard to get me back. He has lost me somewhere. With Nutty, I don't know...it isn't just sexual, there is a huge emotional connect."

Was Tara losing her mind? She felt out of control. *I wish I could have both!*

"You know right, that if Ranvir finds out about Nutty, you are going to be in big trouble. Infidelity is a serious thing. Though you haven't slept together, but you know in your heart, this is cheating. Women who cheat do so because they are looking for a connect. For a man, it is all about the catch and keeping the game 'on'. If Ranvir gets to know, it will be the end of your marriage."

Tara had so much anger inside that she retorted, "Naina, why is it that there is so much tolerance for a man who cheats? Why is it that society is more forgiving toward a man if he cheats on his wife? But for a woman, who is also human, it's unforgivable? When will men understand that emotions are what drive a woman and that's all I damn wanted."

Naina agreed, "Tara, it's like preaching to the choir. I am not disputing anything you are saying. I'm just warning you.

It is all frustrating...the double standards that we live in. But it is what it is..."

Tara was clearly distraught and needed to let go, "Anyway, you are right. I better speak to Nutty and put a stop to this whole thing."

Over the phone, she broached the topic with her mum and was surprised to get her reaction. Her mum lived in a different era where being unfaithful to your husband was largely considered an anathema. She kept reiterating that Ranvir was a good husband and that Tara should give him time. "He has never cheated on you. From what I hear nowadays, that is a big thing."

Tara felt even more agitated after speaking to her mum; she was in no mood to fit into the social stereotype of the forgiving Indian woman. Currently, she wanted to live for herself and be anything but the 'good' wife.

By that evening, Tara wanted to stop thinking about herself. Putting aside her problems, she went over to hang out with Naina. She wondered about her life, "I know I have been absorbed with my own stuff, how are things with you?"

"I'm in a good space. Taking control of my life," Naina laughed. "You know if I was falling apart, I would have been sitting with you over a few bottles of wine, right?"

Tara smiled as she let Naina continue, "To expect a man to look after you seems so ridiculous. I like the control I have over my own life now. I realise that I had been in denial about taking control of my life and had given the strings to Rahul to pull at will. You know, I don't need to be rescued any more,

I can rescue myself. And the best part is that Aseem or no Aseem, I feel fine."

"Whoa Naina! Atta girl! I'm so proud of you. You seem to be on the right path. Can't imagine, it's the same Naina."

"Ya ya, shut up!" Naina laughed and rolled her eyes.

The following weekend, Tara met Nutty for a swim. The pool had just re-opened after the winter season and it was her first swim for the summer. They were standing at the shallow end of the indoor pool and Tara seized the moment to break the news. "Ranvir is coming back to Delhi next month—for a fortnight—to work things out."

She looked at him; his expression didn't change. He looked at her, "So? What does this mean, Tara?"

"Nutty, I have very strong feelings for you. But I can't be with you. It is actually the oldest cliché amongst all clichés. But, I have to give my marriage a chance, fight for my family. I owe it to Neil. I want you in my life but how is that fair to anyone? You? Ranvir? Neil? Me? Who benefits from this?"

She looked at him, sadness in her eyes. *Dammit, I don't want to do this… I don't want to leave you!*

He was quiet for a long time and then he laughed, in a self-disparaging way, "Ha ha! This is the story of my life—always engaged in a cliché and nothing else to go by." He got out of the pool, "Tara, you do what you have to do. You know where I live and you know where to find me."

Tara hurried out of the pool and got dressed. She waited for him by his car. He came out to the parking lot, freshly showered, in a casual hoodie and jeans. He stopped for a moment before he slowly walked towards the car. He came to the driver's side, where she stood. She turned to face him. She didn't say anything, she could feel the tension. It was as if a current was drawing the two closer. She pulled him close and pressed her body against him as she kissed him. She kissed him hard. *He has to know how I feel now… My heart and head are not on the same platform.* He turned and had her against the car in seconds. The kiss deepened; the passion was beyond control now. He explored her mouth and it felt hot. She grabbed him tight as he moved into her body. Closer. So close that they could fit into each other's frame. She arched her back and he moaned. His hand slid down her back and he pulled her closer. It was rough, it was urgent. It was brilliant. They kissed like they were a bunch of horny college kids.

She knew this would end once she pulled away. It was her way of saying many things at once. She finally came back to reality and pulled away. They were breathless. She looked him in the eye, "You are not engaged in a cliché. You are important to me. I just have to do this." He stepped away from the car and nodded. She squeezed his hand before letting it go and slowly walked away into the night.

9

Beginning Again

Aseem's trip to Delhi had been a great break for Naina. It was like peeling off layers and finding something new. It was very refreshing. Aseem told her about his home in Alibagh and had invited her for a family wedding there. They were in a lovely space of getting to know each other.

She learnt about the family he had adopted in Delhi over eight years ago. He took care of their home expenses and the children's education. Naina was very touched by this dimension. At first, she did not believe him, till she met them. They were a sweet, humble lot, who seemed to adore Aseem. He told her about his Delhi education and his friends, his work, his likes and his dislikes. He was very passionate about environment-friendly work projects, and she respected his enthusiasm for something so geocentric.

After he went back to Mumbai, her message box was inundated with Aseem's messages. He knew she was in a state of change. But he was true to his word of 'being there' for her. This was a man who was interested. As if on cue, her phone rang. She took her toast and coffee out into the living room and answered, "Hello."

"Good morning!"

"Good morning, Cliff. How's it going?"

"Someone sounds more chipper than usual at this hour." She could hear the traffic noise in the background. He was on his way to work. He had a rich, deep voice and a very polished accent. Naina liked hearing him speak.

Was it that obvious? Naina laughed. "Just came from my run, getting the day started."

Aseem was not pushy and Naina appreciated that space he gave her. There was no condescending behaviour. There was no need to give any explanation; it was a platform of fair give and take. Aseem aided her self-restoration by just being there. *What more can a woman ask for? I am not naïve to know that every relationship starts off with this sort of interest—the 'honeymoon' phase. I know when the comfort zone sets in is when one actually knows about real compatibility.* But Naina found herself receptive to him and willing to explore. She wanted to arrive at that 'comfort zone' with Aseem.

Aseem said, "Can I make a suggestion on something that might not be my business? And in that spirit, you can totally say, 'It is not your business, Aseem!'"

"It is not your business, Aseem! Ha ha."

He was reluctant, seemed a little nervous as well.

"I'm kidding. Go on," she encouraged.

"Well, your work situation is pathetic. There is no point in hanging on there anymore. It is a good thing you have decided that you are done with your relationship. Yes...yes, it is good for me too! But what I was thinking is that you got great work experience. There are a lot of industrial houses in Mumbai and they do have relocation needs. It is a good business here as well. So, is there something tying you down in Delhi really? Why don't you... Why not find a job at one of the firms here in Mumbai and move?"

"Move to Mumbai?" Naina said, surprised. *Now, where did that come from?*

"Ya... It isn't a bad city. It's actually a great life when you aren't a struggling newcomer. And you are far from it. You can rent a nice apartment in Bandra—the happening, youngish space of Mumbai."

"Well, I am... Well, I never... I have never thought about leaving Delhi."

"Think about it... And you know what the bonus is? We can finally be in the same city."

"Hmm...that sounds like quite the bonus," she thought out aloud.

And that is when the wheels were set in motion. Within a week, Naina had hit the HR consultancy firms and lined up interviews in Mumbai. She took a week off from work. She didn't owe Rahul any explanation, but as an employee, 'holiday' was the reason she gave.

Later, that same evening, Naina sat in her balcony. There was a nice breeze, a perfect April evening. She was thinking about Aseem and how he made her feel...well, nice. And it was such a contrast to her exes. Rahul never made her feel 'nice'. He made her feel a lot of things that swung on extremes from delicious excitement to crazy lows. Never did 'nice' come up when she thought of what she had felt with men from her past. But maybe it was because she met Aseem online. It made it easy for her to just be.

Naina got up and walked into her open kitchen. She poured herself a glass of wine and perched on the stool by the kitchen counter. She sat there, lost in her thoughts, for a long time. She replayed many moments she spent with Rahul. It was a good and bad deck of memories. She thought about Aseem, how he cared about the small stuff. She realised now that made her happy. 'The small stuff.' The 'how was your day?' or 'are you okay?' or 'did you eat?'

Naina felt her resolve about her pride had gotten fierce. She knew she wanted respect above everything else and at all cost. *If you are not capable of respecting me, you can fuck off.* That was her motto now. *I dare to live life as an individual.*

Naina was also conscious of the fact that Aseem and she were on some sort of a journey. Things were going at a pace Naina was comfortable with. She was in control of her own life. And though it felt selfish at times, it felt saner than ever before. This wasn't her 'rebound', this was a change in her *modus operandi*. And she felt strong and good.

After three odd glasses, she felt like letting her hair down. Naina logged on for a chat with Aseem. He was about to call it a night, but Naina was in a mood to play the 'temptress', and coaxed him to stay. Wondering what the game of luring with him would be like, she decided to tease him.

> **(12:23 am) Temptress 007:** So tell me Cliffhanger... how do you engage a lady beyond talk?
>
> **(12:23 am) Temptress 007:** i am a few glasses of wine down and am wondering what your game plan would be...
>
> **(12:24 am) Cliffhanger:** well, let the game play out, right? Planning never works
>
> **(12:24 am) Temptress 007:** so play with me...

(12:24 am) Temptress 007: :)

(12:25 am) Cliffhanger: I have been! There should be slow dance though

(12:25 am) Temptress 007: lol

(12:25 am) Temptress 007: so how would you step it up?

(12:26 am) Cliffhanger: ah well... for starters... I'd take it offline entirely!

(12:26 am) Temptress 007: not now...

(12:26 am) Temptress 007: let's play here. Tell me...

She was being playful and he picked up on her mood. She loved this banter.

(12:25 am) Temptress 007: so how would you step it up?

(12:26 am) Cliffhanger: a drink in our hands, low lighting, cushions thrown around ... a slight breeeeze blowing in from the balcony. Sitting close as music wafts in, smell of the sea lingering...

(12:27 am) Temptress 007: mmm... sounds nice... then?

(12:28 am) Cliffhanger: there's the usual small talk, but there's a palpaple current in the air. enough to get the buzz just right

(12:28 am) Temptress 007: I like the buzz

(12:29 am) Cliffhanger: so you make the usual excuses about it getting late, but... you don't get up to go anywhere

(12:30 am) Cliffhanger: i pour another drink despite your weak resistance

(12:30 am) Temptress 007: mmmm...

(12:31 am) Cliffhanger: the flirtation is heavy. The tension in the air... we want each other... BAD

(12:31 am) Temptress 007: you are good... ha ha! ... it's headed in the right direction

(12:32 am) Cliffhanger: you keep your drink aside casually, and I reach out to you. putting my hand behind your waist, I pull you closer till our lips meet

(12:33 am) Temptress 007: You want this?

(12:33 am) Cliffhanger: you don't?

(12:34 am) Temptress 007: That is not an answer to my question...

(12:35 am) Cliffhanger: yes, I do

(12:36 am) Temptress 007: i like that

(12:36 am) Temptress 007: Then?

(12:37 am) Cliffhanger: your lips part as I explore you. Slowly at first, yet the hunger is real

(12:38 am) Temptress 007: :)

(12:38 am) Cliffhanger: your body stiffens up in the tension of the moment... I pull you closer till you ease up, slowly falling into my arms and against my body.

(12:39 am) Temptress 007: How do we feel up close?

(12:40 am) Cliffhanger: Your body is so warm against mine. I can feel every inch, every curve of you with every breath you take

(12:40 am) Temptress 007: And I can feel yours, heaving against mine... strong and sinewy

(12:40 am) Temptress 007: Making me respond to your touch

(12:41 am) Cliffhanger: oh yes! What else would you like me to do, my lady?

(12:41 am) Temptress 007: No, you are telling this story...

(12:41 am) Cliffhanger: ok... we continue kissing as my arms reach around you

(12:42 am) Cliffhanger: feeling the fabric of your dress, the feel of your skin

(12:43 am) Cliffhanger: i continue to explore you... moving from the lips on to your cheeks, your neck and leaving my imprint there. My hands are searching... exploring... under your dress... teasingly headed up in the right direction...

(12:43 am) Temptress 007: You like to take it slow...

(12:43 am) Cliffhanger: I like foreplay

(12:43 am) Temptress 007: I like it too

(12:44 am) Cliffhanger: Hahaha... and that was the trailer. Darling, enough for now, I think... I know you are driving me crazy... You are sending me off to a lonely bed. I leave you with that. I can't wait to take this offline

(12:44 am) Temptress 007: :) Thanks for the preview. I look forward to catching the whole scene. Till we meet xx goodnight Cliffhanger

"Oh my god! How drunk were you? You were this bold?" Tara said in amusement, as she went through the conversation on Naina's phone the next day. She got regular updates from her friend and was happy that Aseem sounded so good. Above all, Naina had lost that drained-out look she had when she was with Rahul. *I am glad she hasn't fallen back into the same old destructive pattern with him. Bloody low life, selfish bastard used her at convenience,* Tara thought as Naina found a parking spot.

"Well, darling," Tara said, getting off the car, "you definitely look like your spirits are high. And if this is the online conversation, I think you can expect fireworks during your trip to Mumbai! I am so happy for you."

Naina and Tara walked into their regular salon. It was their day to indulge in some much-needed pampering for the soul. They settled in, "Can you ask Meeta to shape my eyebrows please?" Naina said to her manicurist.

"Oh, cleaning up for Mumbai!"

"Shut up, cleaning up, full stop. It looks like I have an extra set of eyebrows!"

As she went through the eyebrow cleaning, Tara and she chatted about the upcoming Mumbai job interviews and her date. They agreed that Naina's date should start at the iconic bar at the Taj Mahal Hotel before anywhere else.

"Now that's a good start!" Naina exclaimed as she checked out her perfect eyebrows in the mirror. "Man, I got cut at a few places. It's like she went to war on my face!"

Tara laughed, "The humour is creeping back in...I like it! I thought I had lost you somewhere between 'bullshitville' and 'heartache town.'"

Naina and Tara zoned out as their manicure and pedicure session started. Sharing a pampering space, they drifted in and out of conversation. Naina sank back into her chair and closed her eyes. By default, Naina reflected on the time gone by with Rahul and how the pain existed but didn't matter anymore. *Even this default thinking of him has reduced drastically. What a relief!*

"You want a coffee?" Naina snapped back to her present with Tara's question.

Naina shook her head, "They say, every relationship changes you and the pain doesn't go away...it fades. You get used to it. Life will never be the same again, and that is a good thing. I now get what that means."

Tara encouraged her friend to get it out of her system, "Hmmm?"

"When I think about Rahul, it is bittersweet. The one I wanted to be with showed me who not to be with in the future. You know?"

Tara understood Naina's thought; she had seen her friend struggle. She took a sip of her coffee and looked at Naina, "I am so glad to see you like this. I was worried you would be stuck in the 'Rahul vortex' forever. But you talking about Rahul in the past is remarkable." She hesitated, "Naina, he didn't deserve you, your love or your loyalty."

"This is not a rebound." Naina stated out loud.

"No silly! It is the first time in your life that you are clear about what you want. It is an adult decision." Tara reassured her.

Aseem had tremendous respect for Naina. *He is the kind of person you should aspire to be with,* she told herself. And it was the sheer stand of clarity of what she really wanted in life, garnished with this respect, that made Naina confident. She pulled through after cutting off Rahul from her life. It was not easy; years spent with someone brings its own see-saw reactions, but she was going to get what she wanted—happiness.

She looked over at Tara and smiled, "My instinct is telling me that whatever is happening is for the good."

The next morning, Naina was off to 'holiday' in Mumbai.

10

Date in Mumbai

"Ladies and gentlemen… Welcome to Mumbai's Chhatrapati Shivaji International Terminal." Naina woke up from her two-hour long snooze. She put on her gloss and kajal. She was ready. She was lucky to have got calls from two leading relocation companies in Mumbai and jumped at the opportunity.

Naina had two interviews lined up over the next three days and then a weekend with Aseem. She was excited and nervous. She left the airport and an hour later, she was at the Taj Mahal Hotel. She loved staying at heritage hotels, especially this one. It was so grand and the staff always treated guests like royalty. After the check-in, she headed to the poolside restaurant to grab a quick bite. Luckily, her first interview was at a corporate office located near to the hotel. It was convenient, given the Mumbai traffic situation.

She sat down and ordered a grilled ham sandwich. She was famished. It was 3:30 pm. She had an hour before her interview. She went over her résumé, thought about her work experience and switched to business mode. Her phone rang. She picked it up with a smile.

"Hello gorgeous, welcome to Mumbai!"

She smiled, "Mr Cliffhanger! I thought you were in meetings till 7 pm. This is a surprise call."

"Well, I am in meetings till then, but I ducked out in between to call you. How was the flight?"

"It was great. I slept through most of it."

"All set for the first interview?"

"Yes, I am."

He sensed she was tense, "Don't be nervous. You will do just fine."

"Thank you."

"Look, I gotta head back in, but I will come by after work. We can get a drink at the lounge and then I want to take you to my local favourite for a bite. Is that cool?"

"Sounds like a plan. See you."

Naina felt relaxed. Confident. She was ready to take on this interview, and this time with Aseem too. She went back into her work zone and prepared for the interview.

An hour later, Naina sat with the director of the firm at a conference room. "Naina, thanks for coming in. That's quite a distance you have travelled to meet us."

"Thank you for meeting me," she smiled. She was calm and relaxed. She had always been at ease in a work environment.

"So, you are ready to take on Mumbai? What brings you here?"

"Well, I have worked in the industry for some years now. It has been a great learning curve. I have dealt with relocation of very high-end technology firms and automobile companies. But I feel I am ready to take on a wider spectrum, sector-wise. Add more industries to my portfolio. I would like to work in the start-ups, investment capital firms and financial institution space. So what better place than Mumbai and I couldn't have got a better firm than yours."

He smiled, "Exactly."

The interview went on for another half an hour. Naina spoke about business she would target, and the laid-out projections. She elaborated on overall structure and process models she had worked on. He seemed impressed.

She came back to her room and lay down for a bit. *Okay, I think that went well.* She switched on the TV and surfed channels. She had time before Aseem would show up. She went over to the sideboard and made tea. She got into bed with her hot cup of tea and unwound over an American talk show. She liked watching this talk show, it made her laugh. Also, it gave her a sense of gratitude for all that she had, and gave hope for what she wanted to achieve in life.

An hour later, Naina was dressed. She wore a floor-length casual knit blue dress and delicate flat sandals. She walked into the lounge. Mumbai greeted her with a fine first evening in town. She loved the sea breeze. The view of the sunset was stunning and made her feel rejuvenated and ready to go. *Okay, who am I kidding? I am excited to meet Aseem!*

He came in shortly after, "Hello, my naughty 'lil Temptress! You look nice." He came straight from office—the white shirt with sleeves rolled up and khakis were a giveaway.

"Hello yourself, Mr I-work-so-hard-I-came-straight-from-office!"

"Yes! Sorry Naina, I had a crazy day today. Meetings galore. Normally, it doesn't go beyond two or three meetings. But today we had back-to-back meetings. I sat in on four concept calls and two presentations. Anyway, enough about that! Let's have a drink, shall we? What would you like?"

Naina sensed a change in Aseem. He had an in-control demeanour about him. It was as if he wanted to subtly say, *This is my hometown; let me be in charge here.* It was endearing.

"Well, you had a long day and I had a tiring one. Scotch sounds good to me."

"And to me too." He looked at the server who had approached them, "Two Chivas please. Large. Ice, water, and soda on the side, thank you."

"So? How did it go?" He asked as the waiter left.

"It was great. I think he liked what I brought to the table."

"See? I knew you'd nail it! That's great."

The drinks came, he poured soda for her and handed her the glass. He raised his glass and looked her straight in the eyes. "To new beginnings. Salud!"

The evening was amazing, to say the least. They went to an old Parsi café, where everyone knew Aseem by name. He ordered the most delicious mutton biryani. Naina pretty much 'mmm-ed' her way through the meal. She looked up at him and caught him looking at her in amusement.

"What?"

He smiled, "Nothing. I just enjoy watching a woman relish her meal. You seem to love the food."

"Oh ya! This stuff is just…amazing! Thank you for bringing me here."

"I'm glad you like it, my pleasure entirely. I simply love this place. It has such character because it has been around for ages; it is a Mumbai icon."

After their sumptuous meal, he drove her back to the hotel. Naina had a 10 am interview across town. In Mumbai terms, that meant driving out at 8 am sharp. He was sweet enough to understand.

"Hey, anything to get you to move closer to me?"

"Good night, Cliff."

He leaned in and kissed her gently. It was a wonderful one, not some desperate boy waiting to eat her face and definitely not a nervous one. It felt natural. It was a confident seal as if to declare that he was here with her, for real. Naina leaned back and smiled. Nice, but she didn't want this to go any further. Not tonight.

"And here I thought you had me with your Temptress profile and the little banter we've had online." He laughed, "Good night, Naina."

It was charming. It was a promise of things to come. The night ended as she had hoped. *Bang on, sugar!* she thought, as she got into bed a few minutes later.

The next two days went by quickly as Naina ran about town. The interviews went well. She felt the energy that Mumbai brought. The people were such professionals; they had a pace at work that made everything seem very efficient. She could see herself getting used to this work environment. She was loving it. They say, Mumbai is the Manhattan of India. *Well, it is quite different from the laidback Delhi life... and I think that is exactly what I need.*

Aseem and she met both evenings and ventured out to lively bars followed by chic restaurants. He knew how to have a good time. She enjoyed being out with him. It was the right kind of attention—light conversation with a stir of excitement. He casually took her hand or put his arm around her many times. It felt good. It felt like they belonged to each other in that moment. It felt like finally Naina was on the same platform with someone she was interested in and vice versa. The intimacy shared was just right. There was a spark. The endless chats and phone conversations had enabled a comfort zone between them.

Friday night was here. It was the night both had been waiting for to see where things went. Naina knew she was ready to be together. Something inside just told her that it felt right. She dressed in her little black dress and three-inch heels. *I shall look 'hot' tonight,* she thought as she touched up her gloss and brushed her hair before heading down.

Aseem met her at the lobby. They were going to head to Bandra, near where he lived.

"Wow! You look…beautiful."

She laughed self-consciously, "I am Temptress 007, you know! You don't look so bad yourself, Cliffhanger." He was dressed in dark jeans and a fitted blue dress shirt.

He had a driver. They sat together, holding hands, on their way to Bandra as the radio belted out popular tunes. She was a little nervous about the night. He seemed at ease. He chatted about Mumbai and the areas they drove by. He took her to a trendy bar and grill. Aseem ordered a bottle of Australian Chardonnay. "A fine wine for a fine night with a very fine lady," he toasted. It was a splendid evening. They stood at the patio and enjoyed their first round of drinks before moving to a table. They enjoyed the wine and ordered some seafood appetisers.

Naina loved how Aseem's eyes would almost twinkle when he spoke about work. She spoke about her kids, he knew pretty much everything about them, but he was interested in her life.

"I would like to meet them some day."

"I would like you to meet them too. They are good kids."

The evening progressed with some light banter, flirting, hand holding...the usual first-few-dates sort of status. Two bottles of wine later, they headed to his place. "Good night Shyam, I'll see you in the morning." The driver handed him the keys and called it a night.

They strolled towards the elevator hand-in-hand. They rode up to the 15th floor. As soon as he shut the front door of his apartment behind him, Aseem pulled Naina into his arms and kissed her.

He took her hand and walked through the small corridor into a living room. They sat on the couch and he leaned in, "Care to put our chat into action?"

He kissed her again. It was a long, passionate kiss. Naina's hands were on his chest and he pulled her closer. "Woo!" she exclaimed, as he lifted her in his arms. They laughed. He carried her into the bedroom, "Oh! I have waited for a very long time for you to come to your senses." The room was spacious and the bed was huge. She smiled at him as he put her down and he pulled her close against him.

"I wanted to do this for weeks," he pulled her into his arms and kissed her slowly. His hands travelled to her lower back as hers went around his neck. She closed her eyes. *This feels so good.* His hands went lower and he pulled her closer into him as his kiss deepened. She leaned into him. It was such a delicious feeling. They fit so naturally into that position. *A beautiful fit,* she thought, *god, I love kissing this man.* She kissed him back with urgency and tightened her arms around him. He lifted her dress and his hands moved to the front.

"Oh baby! You are…so ready."

He walked her to the bed as they savoured every breathtaking kiss. He gently lay her down on her back and swiftly undid his jeans button and pulled off his shirt. He was in front of her—bare, beautiful. Their desire mirrored in each other's eyes. He pulled her dress up as she quickly slipped out of it. She lay there in her black and red lace-trimmed underwear and looked up at him.

"Okay," she smiled, happily.

He bent down and kissed her. He held her down while she felt his strong, toned body and ran her hands up and down his back as he explored her with his mouth, while pulling her dainty laces off her. She arched her back as an urgent moan escaped her lips. He navigated lower. His lips exploring as he went along—the full-cup breasts, the taut belly button, and finally 'there'. His mouth covered her and she gasped. Her heart pounded and mind raced, *Oh baby! I need this. I so badly need this!* She spread her legs and moaned into the side of the pillow. It was pure, raw, sexual bliss.

She pulled him back up and kissed him fiercely. He pinned her arms above her with one hand and looked her in the eyes. "Baby, I want you so bad," he said as he entered her. She wrapped her legs around him and pulled him closer, deeper into her. She felt as if she was under a spell, one of extreme pleasure. It was such an intensely sublime moment. They rocked in sync to a rhythm their bodies shared. Naina felt as if they were frozen in a moment described in books—the 'passions flaring' and 'earth shattering' kinds. She was immensely happy.

As she lay spent in his arms, Aseem looked down at her and laughed, "I am pleased with that expression on your face, Temptress. Let me just say you were more than worth the wait." Naina blushed and he heartily laughed as he bent down to kiss her. Naina looked up at him as he stroked her hair. He smiled and kissed her again. It was a soft, tender kiss. They were comfortable. It was relaxed and felt right. *And oh, so good.* They both dozed off in that position.

Next day, noon, they sat together enjoying the sea breeze on his balcony. He lounged on a chair and she lazily sat on his lap, wearing his shirt from last night. A steaming cup of coffee in her hands, a chilled beer in his. It had been a beautiful first night together, and a welcoming morning. They both sat in relaxed silence. His fingers lazily stroked up and down her back. She loved this feeling of belonging. It was as if they had been together for years.

His apartment was a fairly new construction. He gave her a proper tour in the morning. The setting was contemporary, chic, typical of a bachelor pad. It was a contrast to her cosy and friendly home décor, but in a good way. His apartment was unlike normal Mumbai living; there was ample space. The kitchen opened out into a dining area. The living room had a huge TV and bar that dominated the space. The two bedrooms and the living room had balconies. The view from all three balconies was as good as a Mumbai view could get—two sides faced the sea while the other one faced the traffic on the roads.

Her phone rang. She went in to get it, reluctantly getting up from her perfect position. A few minutes later she came out smiling.

"What happened?"

"You know the company I interviewed with on my first day here? They just called and made an offer!"

He whistled, the local 'siti' type whistle and got up to hug her. "I am so happy for you. It is the one you were rooting for, right?"

"Yes! I can't believe it. The company of choice with a super package." She looked up, "What is going on, universe? I am not used to this treatment!" She laughed and quickly messaged Tara. She had to share the good news with her.

He laughed and kissed her. "Well, whatever the other offers may be, you got the one of your choice in hand. And this is reason to celebrate." He went in and came back with a bottle of champagne and two flutes. "We have a lot of celebrating to do. Come here!"

Naina laughed and sat back in his lap. They popped open the bottle and drank to success, online dating and happiness.

Assem put his glass down, "So Naina, I was thinking... this is really too soon...but since you are starting your life here, would you like to start it with me?"

"Ah!... What do you mean?"

"What I'm asking is would you like to move in with me?"

Naina was taken aback and didn't know what to say. She thought to herself, *I like him... I like him lots! But do I like him enough? I don't want love being consumed by lust. I would prefer the love to grow, one step at a time. Do I want to put myself in that space of being with a man? Why can't I, for once, stand on my own feet and feel complete? Do you really want this, Naina? Or do you want to explore being on your own for once in your life?*

"Hey… I'm still hanging in here? Where have you gone?" Aseem's words broke her reverie.

She looked at Aseem and smiled. "As wonderful as that may sound, Mr Cliff, I don't think… I mean…I don' think I am ready for that. Not yet."

"Look at that! My temptress has finally grown wings! I am happy to see you be 'you.'"

They laughed and she kissed him, "For now, let's get breakfast, please? I'm starving."

The next day, Naina got back to Delhi and went into action mode. Being with Aseem made her realise that she was content and happy with her life now.

Naina was afraid that the persona she had built in her head of Aseem of being a chilled out and supportive person might not match the real him. But the past weekend with him in Mumbai was better than she had imagined. She realised she was not playing 'Temptress 007' anymore and that the relationship had gone to the next level.

Naina was now confident about her move. Within a week after coming back from Mumbai, she resigned. The next few weeks rolled out in a mad frenzy. To celebrate the new beginnings, Naina, Tara and Nihal decided that they needed to unwind and hang out together before Naina's final move.

11

Out of the Closet

Naina put her home on rent and packed up her entire life for the movers. Things were changing with the right amount of shaken and stirred feelings within her. Packing with Tara was efficient and quick. After everything was done, Tara and Naina sat on the floor with a bottle of wine and looked around at all the cartons.

"Man! I'm gonna miss you breezing in and out of my house."

"Come on Tara, you know my work will bring me to Delhi a lot. These industrial houses always need presence in the capital. I can't leave you. You are my home."

"Well baby, whenever you come, you stay with me."

"And Tara, whenever you need to get the hell away from your 'super exciting' life, you know you have a home in Mumbai!"

These last few weeks had been a revelation. The rest of the evening flew by over light chatter, a bag of laughs and take-away food. It was a perfect last evening in the city.

As Naina boarded her plane after wrapping up her life in Delhi, she smiled, *Change is coming and it is damn good thing.*

Tara was mostly at home helping Neil stay focussed on his final exams that had just begun. With Ranvir's impending return, she was going through a roller coaster of emotions. She cherished the time spent with Nutty and missed him dearly. She had been prudent enough to realise that if she took it any further, she would be a major part of the reason for breaking Neil's 'home'.

It had been a long time since she had spoken to Nutty. She was coming to terms with it. It had also been a while since she had spoken to Nihal after their Gymkhana meeting. It was sheer coincidence that when she was thinking of him, Nihal sent her a text message, "Hey! Come on Skype. I want to chat. Lots happening...I need to talk!"

Tara replied back, "Such perfect telepathy! Was thinking about you... Will do after 9 pm. Want to settle Neil down, catch you later."

Finally, Tara settled down with her laptop and a bowl of soup. She went on to chat with Nihal.

> **(9:45 pm) Goo-gle:** Long time... How've you been? What's happening with you?
>
> **(9:46 pm) Ubercool:** I've been too busy at work and with Neil. I have been thinking about Nutty a lot... especially since I see Naina and her online life path. But then, there is Ranvir!
>
> **(9:47 pm) Goo-gle:** Ya, you better watch out! Don't want you to get into an emotional mess and hurt yourself, luv.
>
> **(9:47 pm) Ubercool:** hmm, I know. what abt you? how crazy hv you been going lately? Plans on track? Have you manage to find someone interesting online? Thought about Thailand?

(9:48 pm) Goo-gle: No! Not at all... All men want here is sex, no one wants to be just friends... They want just that.

(9:49 pm) Goo-gle: You know that guy I had my incident with? The asshole has been sending me horrible messages here. I think I sould go offline and get into the real world!

(9:49 pm) Ubercool: Well... then all the more reason to head to Thailand, isn't it? The real world awaits you, my darling.

(9:49 pm) Goo-gle: You won't believe it... the kind of shit this guy has been messaging... he says stupid ignorant things like I am not a 'man' I am a 'whore'! He abuses me, calls me a 'chakka' and all that.

(9:50 pm) Ubercool: Uff! So disgusting. What an asshole! I pity people who are so hell bent on ignorance

(9:50 pm) Goo-gle: Ya! ignor-anus hahahaha

(9:50 pm) Ubercool: mad! ... he's not worth it

(9:51 pm) Goo-gle: I know, I know... bt what do i do! So many messages. It's just rattled me, you know... people can be so hurtful

(9:51 pm) Ubercool: Ignor-anus bastard indeed! No don't even think of it, he is just sick. Block him from your profle. You'll meet somebody... just have patience... go through this sex operation thingy

(9:52 pm) Goo-gle: Yes. i'm staying away from the online space... I don't want people trying to rape me... I have blocked him

(9:52 pm) Ubercool: Absolutely... Delhi is full of whackos

They chatted for a while. Tara calmed Nihal down. He was serious about the sex-change operation. More adamant... in fact, more than ever, NOW.

> **(9:55 pm) Goo-gle:** I spoke to few people who have already been through a Sex Reassignment Surgery. They are all recommending this hospital in Pattaya. I am trying to speak to the doctor there.

Tara was so pleased to hear that he was finally taking steps to own up to who he really was. She encouraged him.

> **(9:56 pm) Ubercool:** Yup. do all your research. I have a cousin working for an NGO, I'm sure she would know of an NGO that could help. let me get back to you, meanwhile you stay cool. Life has a way of sorting itself out. Everything comes a full circle.

A few days later, Nihal called Tara. He was still upset, but it had shaped his decision.

"I have made up my mind, I'm going ahead. It's high time, I can't live like this."

"That is great news, Nihal!"

"By the way, I spoke to my sister, I told her I want to give myself a chance and that I am serious about the surgery. My sister, bless her, says she will come with me for my sessions with the therapist. She is an angel. I am lucky to have her and you support me through this. Will you also come over, Tara? I know it is not your place, but you are a mature person. And maybe, you will handle my parents better."

"Of course, I will be there, sweetheart. But do you think it will really help? I am a stranger after all."

"I know, but I don't think my sister and I can do this alone. Please?"

"Of course, I will be with you all the way."

"JUST GET THE HELL OUT OF MY HOUSE!" Nihal's father shouted. He was seething.

Nihal simply stood there, frozen. Tears were streaming down his face as he tightened his grip on his sister's hand.

Nihal had come clean in front of his father. "Pa, I am a woman trapped in a man's body. I am a transgender."

It was done; a simple sentence that had a nuclear impact on his family. Nihal's father, Mr Sharma, looked pale as a ghost. He had no inkling what the brother-sister duo had wanted to talk about, along with their 'middle-aged' friend. He was uncomfortable to begin with and was shell shocked when he heard it. Anger took over as his first reaction, "You are what? A 'hijra'?"

"No Pa…they are different. I am, and have always been, inclined to be a woman as a person. I don't have any confused organs."

"These are all modern day notions. Where have I failed you as a parent? You are confused and will grow out of it! We should go to a pandit and find a remedy through some prayers and 'havans'! This feeling will pass and you will become 'normal' again."

"But Pa..." Nihal was cut off by him.

"Are you aware that no one will take you seriously once they know you are a transgender? You will be socially isolated, without a family, friends and any relationships! How will you be able to keep your job?"

"But Pa, I have always dressed up as a woman. Whenever you and mom were away, I use to dress up in Choti's clothes. I found peace then. I have always wanted to be a woman. I identify with being a woman. I cannot think of myself as a man. Even as a child, I use to love dressing up as a girl for all the plays in school. I loved the tights, the fluffy dresses. It's not abnormal, Pa. It's my sexual preference, right from the time I understood myself."

Mr Sharma cringed and turned towards his daughter and shouted, "How could you let your brother come to this? Why?"

"How could I see my brother going through the trauma of this dual existence, day in and day out, Pa?" said Nihal's sister.

Tara had been a mute spectator till then. She spoke up, "Mr Sharma, can't you see how hard this is for Nihal? He is struggling with who he is and his love for you had not made him come clean till now. Can you imagine bottling up so many emotions inside? Can you imagine what he has gone through till now? He had bottled everything inside him till now, fearing you, society and the predictable reactions. But for how long will he live a life of denial?"

"He should rather have taken this to his grave than kill me now," said Mr Sharma.

Nihal's mother was crying unconsolably, seeing her child in such an emotional state. "What are you saying, Manoj?" she looked beseechingly at her husband. "Look at him. How does this change who he is to us? He is our baby. Can you imagine what he has been going through?" She looked at Nihal and choked, "And imagine he didn't say anything about this to us for all these years..."

Tara piped in, "Mr Sharma, a parent's happiness lies in seeing their children happy. I have a son, and I know what happens to me when he has a fever. It is upsetting. This is life altering. Can't you not see what he is going through..."

Mr Sharma turned to Tara, his voice stern and raised, "With all due respect, Ma'am, this is none of your business. This is my family matter and I will solve it my way. You have no idea what a let down this...this rascal is! Please leave us to ourselves."

Tara turned to go and as she made her way out of their home, she placed a comforting hand on Nihal's shoulders, and said, "I am waiting outside."

Mr Sharma turned towards Nihal, and shouted, "If you want to change into a woman and all this nonsense, know this... YOU ARE DEAD TO ME. GET OUT!"

"But Pa..."

"SHUT UP. You are an embarrassment to me. You are a deceiving, manipulating liar. And well done...you have managed to shame me in front of the whole world."

Nihal's sister, Namrata, who had been quiet so far, held her brother's hand in support and said, "You are more bothered about people than your own son's strife. Who the hell are these people? When did they become more important than us?"

"Keep quiet, Choti! You don't know anything about these things."

"I know enough to know that my brother is scared. I know that he wants to be himself and has undermined his happiness time and again so as not to let 'you' down. And I know that I can't stand him suffer anymore. And I also know that these so called 'people' you care about, don't care a damn!"

"Choti! Stop it!" her mother pleaded.

"Come on Mom, you know. You have known all along. You just didn't want to do anything about it because of Pa!"

Mrs Sharma slapped her daughter and said, "Choti! Stop!"

But Namrata couldn't be bothered. "We should be able to work through this, listen and respect his needs. All he needs is to be accepted, feel safe and loved." She was sobbing more out of helplessness.

"All of you can say what you want. This...thing..." pointing towards Nihal, "is dead for me. Get out of my house! Now! I don't want to have anything to do with you. I did not raise you to be this! GET OUT!"

Nihal's sister was about to say something, but he held her hand and pulled her back, "Choti, stop." He was too upset. He spoke in a barely audible voice, "We knew this would happen. I just hoped for a miracle."

Addressing his father, Nihal said, "Okay Pa, I will leave. Maybe someday you will be able to forgive me for owning up to who I am. I hope that time comes soon."

Mr Sharma stormed into his bedroom and slammed the door shut.

Nihal gave his mother and sister a hug as they all sobbed helplessly. "Choti, go with your brother to Kamla Aunty's house. I think it is best to let your father be for now. I will stay here to make sure he calms down. You know how his blood pressure fluctuates."

She turned to Nihal, sobbing, "I am so sorry, my darling. I always knew you were suffering but never had the courage to stand..."

She hugged him, "I don't care who you are. You are my baby. You will always be...I am sorry for all you have had to go through." She held him tight. "Go! I love you." She composed herself and wiped her tears and then Nihal's as she held his face gently, "Be yourself. Take care and I want to know everything going on at all times."

"I love you, Mom. I hoped for a better..."

Tara was waiting downstairs. She could tell it was a huge struggle for Nihal's mom. She looked up at the balcony at Nihal's mother.

"Come on, sweetheart. I will drop you to your aunt's place."

"Thank you, Tara. I am sorry about the way..."

"Please! Don't apologise. I understand completely. And don't worry, Mr Sharma is a parent. I understand he would have had some expectations out of you, Nihal. It will be tough to come to terms with this, but he will, I guess, over time. You really should be proud of yourself and your courage to face the truth."

Sitting in the car, Tara could see that Nihal was totally shattered and lost. Looking out of the window, he said, "My father just threw me out of my house...just like that... I am not surprised. I expected this... He is just... He belongs to another era."

Tara let him speak.

"I am going to be fine. I am relieved actually..." Nihal sighed. "Someday he will come around. He has to..." He looked over at Tara, "Right?"

She glanced over at him and smiled. "Time... I hope so."

Namrata spoke from the back seat, "Turn right here, Tara."

"Namrata, may I offer you some unsolicited advice?" Tara questioned.

"Sure... you are family to us now, Tara."

"I know you are angry at your folks. But you are still living with them. This is hard on them as it is on Nihal and you. Just be patient. This was a lot for your father to take in... Give him time. But in the meantime, don't make it a miserable time for yourself and them at home."

Nihal turned to Namrata, "Choti, I love you for everything you have done for me. You are my guardian angel. But we have to understand that Pa needs time to digest all this."

"I love you too... Listen, we are with you, Mom and I. You have to know that. Kamla Aunty is a sweetheart. She too will be supportive. Bhai, promise me you won't shut us out."

"She is right, Nihal. You should focus on all the support you have... We are all here. Whatever you need us for. Download on 'us'!"

"Thank you. Thank you, guys. Tara, you've been extremely supportive ."

"Oh shush! I love you, silly! And I am going to hold your hand through this change all the way. You are going to be just fine...and happy."

And at that, a small smile cracked at the corner of Nihal's lips. He just needed to feel loved after this feeling of banishment.

They reached Kamla's place. "Thanks Tara. I will take it on from here."

"You sure? I can come in with you."

"No no... Kamla Aunty is Mom's best friend, more like a soul sister, from her school days. She is like a second Mom to me. We will be fine."

Tara hugged Nihal, "Love you, kiddo! And super proud of you!"

A couple of days had gone by, and Tara was a little anxious because she hadn't heard from Nihal. Normally, he would send a text message or call. Finally, unable to stay away, she called him.

"Hey, how are you? Are you okay?"

"Ya...umm... I am... I just needed some space to internalise and am just settling into Kamla Aunty's house. She is such a darling. Choti has been visitng me regularly, shifting my things and making me as comfortable as possible."

"Er... You know what Tara..."

"Go on."

"Mom had been aware that I was different. She was relieved for me to come out in the open."

"How is your dad now?"

"He has very little information or knowledge about this issue, so I totally understand his reaction of shock and disgust."

"Poor guy! But you are an adult, Nihal."

Tara understood Mr Sharma's reaction being a parent herself, but then, she was more aware, open to new thoughts, ideas and more accepting.

"I will give him time, Tara. I don't have a choice. But it is my life and I am going to go ahead with the decision I have taken. I feel so relieved having it all out in the open to the people who matter to me the most."

"I want to meet you, when should I see you? Should we meet in the evening?"

"Ya…we can… Why don't you come around 4 pm? We can meet at a coffee place nearby. Don't want to impose on Kamla Aunty more than I have to…"

Tara drove down to meet Nihal. To cheer him up, on a whim, she carried a brand new piece of lingerie that she had bought recently from a reputed store.

"Hi baby!" Tara hugged Nihal. "Look what I got for you!"

Nihal opened the packet and flaunted his gift with a flourish, "Oh! It's beautiful! I can't wait to wear it! Thanks, Tara! You are such a doll."

"My pleasure love… How are you feeling?"

"I am okay… Anxious, but fine. I feel ready to take on the next step."

"I understand why your father reacted the way he did. It is natural. Most parents would be confused and in denial… they would want to sweep it under the carpet thinking this can't be happening to my son. But don't worry, your dad will settle down."

"I know. My sister spoke to him recently. She handled it beautifully. She told dad that there were a lot of people who were going through this in India, and that it was all on the Internet. She explained to him that I am not confused and I had been like this for as long as she could remember. She also told my folks that I was absolutely clear that I wanted to go in for a sex-change operation and that if not any of them, she will see me through it."

Tara smiled, "She surely is a gem! What wonderful support, Nihal."

"Yes. I was overwhelmed by her strength to help me. She is just wonderful."

"You are blessed, sweetheart! And here you thought you were all alone. Rubbish!"

"Nihal, you know I was reading on the Internet about Kusum, a transgender who went through this operation and now runs an NGO in India. How about if we talk to her? She would be able to give you some insight into the whole thing. Also, you should check out similar support groups. People who have already been through this... Speak to them, it'll help you prepare."

"Yes, Tara. I will look into all that. Now, I am focussing on what is required for my Thailand recce. Just want to go to the best doctor available."

"Wait! I have done some homework for you." Tara opened her notes on her phone, and continued, "There is a certain Dr Peru in Thailand. Apparently, he is world-renowned for these operations, and his clinic is in Chonburi. He does about 8,500 surgeries every year! People come from all over the world and his clinic has the most advanced medical facilities available. I am so excited! I have already written to them hinting about your visit."

Nihal's eyes moistened, "You are awesome. I was plain lucky when I hit on you online."

Tara laughed, "Ya ya...now listen! They have sent me details about the surgery, high quality procedures and more. Basically, there are two major surgeries, SRS (Sex Reassignment Surgery) which is for the actual sex change and FFS (Facial Feminising Surgery). And the good news is...since you have already started your process here with a psychologist and have started your hormone pills, you can get everything done in two weeks, recuperate for another two weeks. So darling, you can get back home in one month... maximum, two months...as Niharika."

Nihal's face lit up with excitement, "My dear, dear Ubercool! What would I do without you? But what about the cost of all this?"

"The cost depends on the two different kinds of vaginas. They can invert what you have there; it is called a Penial Inversion. Or, they have a procedure, where they use a piece of your colon to recreate a vagina. If I were you, I would go with the colon one. Certain complications are lessened with that and I am made to understand that it feels more real. And the cherry topping, no pun intended, is that you actually climax!"

Both Tara and Nihal laughed. He asked, "How much will this cherry topping cost me?"

"The entire thing should cost you under 12 lakhs. That includes a chauffer pick up from the airport and a drop back as well!"

"Hmm…that's a lot! I have around six lakhs saved. How will I manage the rest?"

"Okay, I have an idea. Your hormone pills have already kicked in quite well. You can pull off being a woman already when you dress as Niharika. So why don't you first get the Sex Reassignment Surgery? Save money and a year later, go in for the Facial Feminisation Surgery."

"Also, the advantage of that is, by then, I will be clearer on what aspect of the FFS I want."

"Oh ya!… I didn't think of that." Tara laughed.

"I'm so glad we met. I feel so positive now."

"On that note sweetheart, I am going to leave. Neil will be back from his soccer practice soon."

"Thanks, love. I want to do this real bad. And I am sure it will all work out for me."

12

An Emotional Connect

Life was moving fast, the suddenness of Ranvir's arrival caught Tara by surprise. Ranvir was in town trying to wind up his current assignment and get a new one in Delhi. Tara heard him discuss his relocation plans with his office staff and it looked like his plans to return to Delhi were finally coming through.

Apparently, the whole Neil incident had really shaken Ranvir up and he was genuinely worried. It had been three days post his return and Ranvir was making a sincere effort to mend things with Tara.

At the same time, Naina had landed in Delhi to attend a young entrepreneurs' conclave. She was representing her company in Delhi and this gave her a perfect opportunity to stay with Tara. She had been away for about six months; it had been a long time since the friends had met and the house was buzzing with activity.

Naina walked in; all this felt so familiar, almost like homecoming. She hugged Tara, "I'm so glad to be back in Delhi here with you. Where is Ranvir?"

"He should be back soon."

"Why are you looking so tense?"

Tara rolled her eyes, "It's a long story. Let's get a cup of tea first."

"By the way Nains, you look good, you know, you have an air of confidence around you… Hmm, I like it."

Naina broke into a smile and said, "Tara… It's 'Mumbai Meri Jaan'; the city treats me well and the men even better."

Tara asked, "Yes of course, how has our virtual man Aseem been treating you?"

Naina smiled back and as they settled on the couch for the evening, she said, "You know, Aseem is a great guy, but, I am in no hurry. I no longer feel the need to cling to a relationship. I wish I could have gotten here some other way, but my break-up with Rahul actually helped me to understand myself. Today, I am happy to just be." She looked over at Tara, "So far so good! Aseem is amazing, but I am not hanging off a 'cliff' for him. Ha ha! I do have my fingers crossed, let's keep it at that."

"Naina, you have come a long way from your miserable Rahul days."

Naina sipped her tea and looked at her friend. She could sense that Tara needed to talk, "Forget about me, Ranvir is in town and is planning on moving back to Delhi? Are you happy?"

Tara sighed, "I don't know. Now that I am getting what I want… I am thinking is it really what I actually want?"

"But how are things with you guys? And what about Nutty?"

Tara looked at her friend and said with a wry smile, "Hmm, I just don't understand myself. I had called it off with Nutty. Whatever there was to call off anyway," she mocked in sarcastic bitterness. "I stopped it from going further, but then why the hell do I find disconnecting with him so hard?"

"I feel torn into two parts like never before. Life is too complicated. Just when I thought that things had reached a dead end with Ranvir, he decided to come back. On one hand, I want my marriage to work out, if not for anything else, for Neil… and for Neil alone. On the other hand, this so-called relationship with Nutty, feeling deeply for him, the emotional connect and not to miss, the spark between us, is driving me nuts. It's so damn complicated. I can't commit to him because of Ranvir, but I can't get Nutty out of my mind."

Tara went over to her cabinet and pulled out her 'for-occasions-only' bottle. This anger needed to be mellowed down with a smooth whisky before Ranvir got home. She brought back a tray of glasses, ice and the single malt and set it down on the coffee table in front of them.

Naina poured out the drinks, clunked two cubes of ice into their respective glasses and held hers upfront and said with much ado, "Cheers to Nutty?"

Tara smiled, "Fine… Whatever… I hate when you tease."

Naina laughed, "Me too. But what to do? Life is stranger than fiction."

Tara never had problems with having men indulge her. She had a ball in her 20s. Ranvir and she were the hot, brilliant, young couple—the new successful kids in town who couldn't do without each other. They dated for quite a while before they decided to get married. Those were the grand days. People used to joke at parties, "The way you two keep hanging out, it seems that you don't see enough of each other at home." Life had come a long way since then. She had reached a situation where she was tempted to stray from her marriage towards this delicious, beautiful firefly of a man.

They sipped their drinks in silence. Tara's monologue continued. She needed this. "I have connected with many men throughout my life—emotionally, professionally. I am not new to this, so why is Nutty not as easy to let go of..."

Naina was sitting on her couch, looking out of the window. She said, "Take it easy, stop being so hard on yourself... Give it time and I'm sure things will get sorted out between you and Ranvir."

Tara retorted in a deadpan voice, "They are both brilliant men. My relationship with Ranvir is important, we have a shared history but we have no connect. Nutty and I are bonded and connected in the now. What a dilemma!"

"Have you ever discussed this with Ranvir?"

"You know him and his work... Neil and I...we faded in the background. We became white noise for him."

"Maybe he has become white noise for you now? Maybe that is why Nutty is even more attractive to you."

Ranvir's car pulled into the driveway, "The prodigal husband returns...I really hope for your sake this whole thing sorts out."

A few minutes later he walked in, "Hi Naina! Good to see you. Been too long. Heard you are up to mischief in Mumbai?"

"How I wish! But yes, just grabbing opportunities. To be honest, I am glad to be in Mumbai."

Tara got up and stretched, "Okay guys, you two catch up. I am off to prepare dinner."

Naina also got up from her sprawled-out position and went in to help Tara.

Over whisky and pasta the three of them had a lot of catching up to do. Finally it felt like old times again.

Tara woke up the next day groggy from last night's drinking escapade. Ranvir was leaving for work. He had tried to reach out to her, but she had feigned a headache. Not entirely untrue considering the overdose of alcohol she had consumed. Tara found herself holding back from Ranvir and her thoughts kept going to Nutty. She thought, *This all-consuming bullshit has to stop. I'm just going to call Nutty today. I can't bear it anymore. I need to talk to him just one last time. This will end soon. I need to hear his voice one last time. I need to say a proper goodbye before I settle down with Ranvir.*

Later in the morning, soon after Ranvir left for work, she checked her watch, "Nutty must be leaving for work now. Good time to chat."

"Hi!" He picked up in three rings and sounded busy, but surprised.

"Hi Nutty, how are you?" a feeble voice came out with great difficulty.

"I am good, sweetheart. How are you?"

"I am fine."

"Hmm…okay. What's going on? How have you been?"

"Hmm…" She had called but didn't know what to say. She was drawing a blank. *Why am I calling him? What will it achieve? It's good to hear his voice. Teenager!* She cursed herself and muttered, "What have you been up to?"

"Well, since you left me, my poor damaged soul felt very lost. I have been busy with a massive project, so luckily that saved me," he laughed, and added, "I have been travelling between Mumbai, Hyderabad and Delhi and we haven't talked for over a couple of months and nine days."

This time Tara laughed at his sarcasm. She felt happy to know that he kept track.

I hate it that he can take it in his stride. I wish I could too... When did the chased become the chaser?

"Yes... I think of you, Tara. More than I would like to admit. What have you been up to? As a matter of fact, I was in Mumbai last week and I thought of you. Was at an art gallery. It was right up your alley." And just like that, for a lark, they picked up from where they left off. It was again the comfortable, light and fun banter that had got them together. To engage with Nutty felt so natural.

Tara wanted to tell him about the turmoil inside her and about Ranvir. She collected all her emotions within and let out a deep sigh, "Well, not much, just busy with Neil, work and the big one—Ranvir."

"He's back?"

"Ya...and it seems like for good. What are you doing today? Is it okay if we meet some time? I need to talk."

Nutty said, concerned, "Are you all right? Hope all is well with you. Why don't you come over for an early evening drink?"

Tara froze. Excitement! Panic! Relief! Joy! Guilt! Guilt... more guilt...even more guilt.

"Let it be! I don't think it's a good idea to meet, especially at your place."

"Come on! I won't bite. I mean...I would like to, but not till you are okay with it. Come on then, it's only a drink. I have this beautiful French red I want to crack open. What say?"

Tara knew she was going to give in. She hesitated for a fraction of a minute. She had been dying to see Nutty. She heard herself confirming, "Sure, how can I say no to a red? What time?" Tara couldn't understand how and why she was so drawn to this person.

"How does 5:30 pm sound?"

"Sounds doable, but not today. Neil is away with his buddies for dinner tomorrow. I am free before Ranvir heads back home from his meeting up in town."

"Cool, see you at home tomorrow."

They hung up. *What just happened? What did I do? Visiting a man I am attracted to...at his house? Wise! Oh, how wise!*

Tara wore her wrap-around dress. A hot pink one with designs all over in subtle shades of reds and pinks. It was wild. It was hot. It was what she was feeling. Her hair was messy and open, the sexy look. It was a casual look. Her gladiator sandals completed the chic look...the carefully-crafted carefree look. She gave herself a once over in the mirror.

She was walking out as she called Naina. "Ya, I am headed out to Nutty's. Shall be home by 7:30 pm. You should be done by then as well? Cool?"

"No, not cool Tara! You are making me nervous. Why are you doing this to yourself? Here is a man who you are interested in. There is a man you are tied down to...they are two different men."

"Ya...it's just a drink, Nains! I don't want to think beyond that."

"Don't 'ya-ya' me!"

Tara couldn't help but laugh at her friend's concern, "I get what you are saying. Ranvir is back now, so this is like a goodbye meeting. I can handle it. That's all."

"Throwing caution to the wind, are we, Ms Tara?"

"Something like that…let's see. Let's not build it up." She stepped behind the wheel and started her car. "Okay, gotta go, love. Let's hope for the best! Ciao!"

"Whatever that calm attitude is… I shall drink some before you get here. Dammit Tara, I am nervous as hell!"

"Ha ha! You mad woman. Okay bye."

She hung up as she drove out of the gate. Tara was surprised at how calm she was about meeting Nutty. She was looking forward to it. It was like a natural step. *Going over for drinks. What's wrong with that?*

In some way, Tara always felt that chatting was not cheating. It was time pass and that helped remove a sense of guilt. But this, she was aware, was way beyond that.

She parked in front of his gate and slowly, as if it was something she did all the time, let herself into the driveway.

A colonial home, Nutty had inherited this mansion from his grandmother. He lived alone in this massive South Delhi house, sprawled over two floors, with a beautifully maintained garden and a long driveway. *Spacious, clean and green,* she thought. She rang the bell and heard Nutty's voice far from somewhere inside, "Coming." He sounded relaxed, happy. He opened the door with a smile.

She smiled back. Her attraction for Nutty had deepened in his absence. Absurd. *Imbecile,* she cursed herself.

"Hello, stranger."

"Hi, Nutty! I hope I am not too late."

"No, no! Bang on time, as always. I was in the kitchen."

Tara got a whiff of the fresh-from-the-oven aroma.

"Come, let's sit."

"Nice house."

"I love it. I spent my childhood here. You know... grandparents and weekends."

"It's lovely." She looked around the room; he seemed to have left it intact with the old, heavy, dark wood furniture, a matching cabinet with glass adorned with shelves of crystal and porcelain pieces on display. A bar area and dining set to match the entire sitting space; it all added to the old world charm of the construction.

"The atrium makes this space look so big."

He looked up, "Ya. My grandfather insisted on it."

All this small talk was just a cover; Tara was nervous as hell. She was being very proper and feeling a bit awkward. Nutty, on the other hand, was completely at ease, lounging next to her in his white linen shirt and light blue linen pants and tan loafers.

She sat back, "So, how have you been? What have you been up to?"

Nutty got up and headed to the bar, "Like I said, work had me going. I am glad you called." He pulled out two long stem goblets and the wine opener. He continued as he opened the wine, "I missed you. I am happy to see you again. But, the bigger question is, are you happy to see me again?" He poured the wine and walked over and handed her a glass. She took it and looked up at him. He smiled, "Well then, cheers to that look."

They sipped the wine. She was sitting at the edge of the sofa. "Yes, I missed you too, Nutty. There. I said it. I mean things are not any different with Ranvir, and we...," she gestured, "are not doing anything wrong... What the fuck man! You and I, we are a good thing, right? And that's all that matters?"

He sat next to her and lounged back, while running his hand up and down her back. "Careful Tara, we will have to agree to disagree. While you are a great companion, you know I want to do all sorts of sinfully 'good wrongs' with you."

Tara felt a delicious current all the way down her back, like she hadn't felt in a very very long time. She leaned back into his arms. They sat there together, sipping the wine, comfortable, yet supremely aware of the growing passion between them. Everything was perfect.

"I better go get that snack platter out before we sizzle into crisps ourselves."

She laughed to overcome her wariness, "Let me help you... You made such an effort."

They strolled into the kitchen hand in hand. She was far from hungry, instead, there were butterflies inside her. She felt empowered and demure at the same time.

A platter of cheese and crackers and a bowl of hummus lay on a tray. He pulled out the veggies from the grill and plated them. He carried the beautiful tray out and set it on the bar counter. She followed him out and sat on the bar stool.

"It smells divine." She took a pepper, dipped it in the hummus and took a small bite. "Mmm... Good job, Nutty! I'm impressed." She was feeling a little more relaxed.

"I'm glad you like it." He got their glasses and poured some more wine. "Thank you. I assume you like the wine too?"

"Uh-hmm," she nodded her head as she took a sip.

Perfect. She was in that familiar yet exciting space again. Nutty made her feel alive. *I haven't felt like this in so long...* It was nice to feel wanted.

Nutty gently pulled her, off the stool, into his arms and kissed her. Tara was startled by the swiftness of the action but it lasted for a fleeting moment before she kissed him back.

Tara leaned into him. Arms around his neck, she entwined her fingers in his soft luxurious hair. He pulled her close, strong arms wrapped around her lower back. His lips covered hers; he tugged gently with his teeth for a moment before he probed further down to her jaw, and slowly down to her neck.

She arched her back and moved her head back slowly. "Nutty..." she moaned.

His kisses were intense and passionate—the deep throbbing kind of kiss; the shatteringly urgent but still gentle kiss; the go-on-for-hours kind of kiss. Tara was on top of the world. It drove her nuts!

They kissed for a very long time. Finally, when they disentangled themselves from each other's embrace, Nutty looked down at her, smiled and pulled her hair off her face and held it back, "*Uff*...woman! You will be the end of me." They smiled at each other. "And you me?" she asked and stated simultaneously. He nodded and took a deep breath as he stepped back. He handed the glass back to her and took a sip from his own. He took her hand and led her to the sofa. She was aware of the madness within her.

"Nutty?"

"Hmm?"

"You know I want to, right?"

"Yes, I can feel it darling. But I am not stupid. I know what coming here meant for you. You broke enough of your own rules for one day."

She was surprised and looked up at him.

"What? You think I don't know what a big deal this is for you and your lines of 'propriety'? Come on Tara. I wasn't going to lure you into my lair and jump on you. I am not some selfish savage. I know better."

"I would love nothing more, you know that."

He groaned. "Please don't say that, it makes it harder than it already is… Pun totally intended!" he looked down.

She laughed. She laughed so hard that she snorted. "Sorry, that was so sexy of me," she said with a smile.

"Look love, I am not a lust-eyed teenager. I am an adult and I will pursue you like one. I know what would happen to you if we made love right now. You would loathe it afterward. You would loathe yourself, and worse, you would loathe me. So till you don't come to terms with where you are in your marriage, I will wait. Oh and you will be so worth that wait." He leaned in and kissed her. "But till then, off you go…"

"Nutty, I am so sorry. I want to…but…I am married. To Ranvir. Ranvir was my focus. And I was his. He remained my focus, but I became that person he distanced from. He completely shut me out. Then you came in. I warmed up to someone. Now we are here. And now he's back. And I just… don't know…anything. Anymore."

"This needs lots of wine, time and patience. I don't need an explanation. You do. Go on…explain it to yourself. Tara, sooner or later you will realise what you want and what you need to do. Till then, no justifications required."

He held her face gently in his hands, "But, do me a favour? Don't suddenly cut me off from your life like this... Can we please resume doing the fun things together? I miss going on walks with you, enjoying an art exhibit together or just catching a movie. Is that asking for too much?"

"I miss you too, Nutty. But these lines, the blurriness... I am so confused." She got up. She had worked herself up again over the dos and the don'ts.

"Okay, stop. Just stop. Think about it. That's all?"

Tara didn't want to leave Nutty but was in a huff. She wanted to head back before Ranvir got home from work. She left shortly after that intimate yet serious conversation.

Tara was driving when Naina called for an update. Tara's insides were feeling all over the place. Her emotions were playing tug-of-war. She pulled up along the kerb to talk.

"Man! He must really like you! Like, 'actually' like you. Think about it! Which man says that?"

"A man who isn't thinking between the legs."

"Oh please! How many men have you known to not have their brains in their balls?"

"Okay, fine. None. But I think this is the difference between single men and divorced men or men who have had live-in relationships. They grow up! They are aware of the realities of women."

"So what do you want to do now?"

"I don't know. I told him I would think about it and that I need to take things slowly. So no frequent calls and no more getting into each other's lives. I need time to figure out things, Nains. I like him, I am attracted to him. But I have a husband. Who is waiting at home!"

"Yes, he is actually. He walked in about five minutes ago." Naina took a sip of her wine, "By the way, Ranvir is a good guy."

"Yes, that is what makes this so annoying. If he was a jerk like Rahul, I wouldn't be in a dilemma."

"Hey... Okay, you are allowed that! But what are you thinking?"

"Well, I am not gonna walk out on my son. As angry as I am for the disconnect between Ranvir and me, I cannot do this to Neil."

"Okay, so let me rephrase this—what do you want to do?"

"Oh man!... What I want to do is..."

Naina giggled like a schoolgirl, "Now we are getting somewhere!"

Tara opened her bag to take out her cigarettes; "Okay, see you in a bit!"

She had a missed call from Ranvir. Tara called him back. She was surprised when Ranvir said, "Hey, where have you been? I've been calling all evening."

She panicked and had a series of overwhelmingly strong emotions that were contradictory. She mumbled something when Ranvir cut her off, "I wanted to ask you out for dinner tonight. Naina's here, so we could go to that new restaurant you have been dying to eat at."

Tara was stunned. She didn't know what to say. He was actually trying to work things out.

This was her moment of reckoning. *What the heck? This is happening too fast. Yes, I need to give Ranvir another chance.*

Tara remembered a quote from Rumi and it suddenly seemed appropriate in this situation, '*Your task is not to seek love, but merely to seek and remove all the barriers within yourself that you have built against it.*'

Life has a way of sorting itself out. Just leave it. Everything will be okay over time. Take each day as it comes.

13

Polyamorous

Come July, Ranvir was back home to stay. He was taking over as the regional director, North India, of an immensely big multinational firm. It was a critical assignment in his career graph. Tara was getting used to Ranvir's move back home. Earlier, she was solely responsible for Neil and ran the house according to her schedule. Now the focus moved to both of them. It was Ranvir's birthday the following weekend. Tara wanted to go all out to make it special for him and decided to pull out all the stops. It was her way of making an effort. *Maybe, this overcompensation is to silence that nagging guilt.*

She planned to throw a grand party for him. The couple would be playing hosts after a long time and Tara had called all their friends and some family members. She wanted it to be a homecoming of sorts for Ranvir and a reiteration of the family as one unit again.

Finally, it was Saturday, the night of the party. Tara was in the living room giving last-minute touches to the house. She had finished decorating with the fresh flowers she had bought. The final touch was the sexy new halter dress that she donned.

Naina had specially flown down all the way to Delhi, from Mumbai, to be part of Ranvir's birthday celebration. Tara was happy to have her join the party planning. Above all, Tara was really excited about Nihal coming over. He was on his way back from Thailand and Tara had been in constant touch with him. He was sounding very excited and upbeat. He had met up with the doctor and with a couple of patients who had already undergone the SRS. Nihal was convinced that he had a fairly high rate of assimilation and that his impending surgery would be a success. Tara was super excited to see him as Niharika.

"Tara, from now on, I have decided to appear in public only as a woman, as Niharika. That's part of the process and is the way ahead for me," Nihal had told Tara in an earlier conversation, when she had called to invite him over.

"I'm so excited. I can't wait for you to come to the party, Goo-gle!"

The guests started pouring in and soon it was a packed house. The chatter in the room was loud, interspersed with laughter, the tinkling of champagne flutes and the music playing to Tara's favourite band, Santana.

It was nice to have all their close friends and relatives over after such a long period of time. She had spruced up her place and she looked around at her handiwork with a sense of pride. The sprawling living room opened into a balcony with a green cover. The classic line of comfortable white contemporary furniture, with the lights turned down, looked great. The impressive Sheffield tableware, an inheritance from her mother, looked grand. Tara looked around and said to herself, *Hmm, Tara, you have quite a lovely house, lady. Great style, I must say*. She giggled, quite house-proud.

The food was being catered by a Japanese restaurant. The elegant selection of dishes was impressive and had been painstakingly handpicked for the guests. Tara was instructing the waiters to bring in the snacks, when Ranvir's oldest friend, Samir, walked in.

"Hi Ranvir! It's been a long time. I'm glad you are back in Delhi." They hugged.

"Tara, you look simply gorgeous." He kissed her on the check and looked over at Ranvir and winked, "Ranvir, how the hell can you leave your lovely wife behind? One day, some lucky bugger is going to whisk her away from under your nose!"

Tara froze with that comment. *Had Samir guessed something?* Suddenly, guilt assailed her like a bolt of lightning. She recovered quickly, and looked Samir in his eyes and smiled contritely, "No such thing, Sam! Sorry to disappoint you, but Ranvir and me are for keeps."

Ranvir looked at her, a bit puzzled by her sharp tone. He put his arms around her and said, "Chill, darling! He's just pulling your leg. I know you only too well, you are incapable of cheating. You hate twisted, underhand liaisons. Sam, buddy, I trust her too much; she would never do this to me."

Tara thought to herself, *Ranvir, your confidence in me is unfounded. If only you knew how confused I feel at the moment. I'm completely torn inside; you would be shocked if you knew what I had been up to behind your back.*

Just then, Neil came to them, "Mom, can dad take me for the soccer match tomorrow? Dad, do you think my team will win the game?"

Ranvir smiled at Neil and said, "We gotta win, champ!" and they exchanged high-fives.

Tara was relieved to have Ranvir back because she could see the impact his presence had on Neil and it was clear that he genuinely missed his father. Ranvir knew exactly how to tackle his raging teenage hormones and had him singing to his tune.

Life had changed with Ranvir back in town. Tara was busy getting life in gear with him. After six years of living in and out, it almost felt like she was getting to know him anew. Tara was beginning to enjoy the bustle in the house. Most importantly, Neil was settling down.

Tara was in the kitchen checking on the snacks. She wanted to be the perfect host and make her friends feel at home. She was watching over the wasabi dip for the sushi platter, when Naina walked into the kitchen with Niharika.

"Look who just walked in!"

"Hey, look at you! Hi gorgeous! I am so happy to see you, Niharika!"

Niharika was wearing a black sheath dress that fell just above her knee and showed off her sexy long legs. Her high stilettos made her a statuesque 5'11". She had highlights in her hair and was sporting a short chic blunt. "You look vavooom, babe!"

"Thank you for inviting me," Niharika hugged Tara. "You have such a stylish house, and what a wonderful party this is."

"Okay, let's go and sit outside for a smoke!" They settled into their chairs on the balcony.

"Hmm… Life seems to have come a full circle," Tara smiled.

"I'm so happy to be here," said Niharika. "Naina, how are things with you?"

"Things are going great. Mumbai is good and Aseem is yum. Ha ha! Work is brilliant. But you are the star of the moment. How was Thailand?"

"I can't tell you how I loved Thailand. I met so many people on the same life journey as me. I found a certain peace in Thailand that I hadn't experienced anywhere else. I might just move there!"

"Are you serious?"

"I can't explain it. People are a lot more human and accepting of transgenders than they are here. It's been good and I think things will work out well for me. And you know what, for the first time in my life, I feel centred and optimistic. And that despair that always hung over me like a pall of gloom, is lifting. You know Tara, I can't thank you enough. I could've never done this without you."

"Oh shush!... It is your life journey. You would be here either way."

"Hey! Now that Ranvir's here, what's happening with you?"

Naina looked at her friend, amused, "Yes, Tara, pray tell?"

Tara smiled. "I am trying guys... A six-year disconnect is not so easy to overcome. Sure, I think about Nutty. We got close so quickly. He got me. Ranvir and I are together, but we have a lot of catching up to do. We were a certain kind back then, and now, we are different from what we were."

Tara paused as if to think things through and continued, "I'm happy to have Ranvir back. I'm truly giving it my best. I am trying not to retreat into a space that brought us here." She smiled. But Tara felt so distant from Ranvir. She had tried putting her heart and soul into making the marriage work but the past kept creeping in.

Naina looked at her, "You know, everything in life moves in cycles. Even experiences—we go through them, they start and end, and they are complete. The trick is to learn from them, to have a better cycle the next time around, not to be afraid to start over, but, to take it in stride. New beginnings are what we should focus on, not on the endings…which, we tend to do a lot."

"Tara, as long as you are in it together, you will pull through. This is why my marriage failed…we were not in it together. Though for me, it was different because I had a husband who was everywhere but with me."

"But how can so many years of being on the fringe be fixed? How can I bury the feeling of resentment that has been building up year after year? Ranvir has been so self-absorbed, will I ever forgive him for being so indifferent to me…so remote and so far away. How will he ever make up for all those lonely years? Can he ever give them back to me?"

She recounted for her two friends, but it seemed like she was reiterating to herself, "Almost a year ago, or maybe a year and a half ago, when I first met Nutty, it was a silly game. It was texting back and forth, light and gentle flirting. It developed into a bit more and then a bit more. Now I just can't get Nutty out of my mind, I feel so attracted to him. I can't get him out of my head and heart." She was not into casual flings, dishonest liaisons or irresponsible behaviour, but then suddenly before she realised it, she was emotionally hooked on to Nutty. She knew it was 'morally' wrong. She also knew that Ranvir would never forgive her.

However, here was the quandary, "I think…well, I know I love Nutty." It felt good to say it out aloud for the first time. She had been feeling like she was going to explode, carrying this thought within. "I don't want to break my marriage because I don't want to let Neil down." The best part of her life was her son…with the smile that melted her heart every single time she looked at him…Neil was the most significant part of her being. What she had was beautiful and to break that would be the biggest mistake and regret in her life.

Plus, Nutty was a single guy. She felt she had no right to press him for a commitment when she herself was still married. He did say to her that they should think of a future together. Yet, given her situation, the thought of breaking up with Ranvir seemed so unfeasible.

Naina took Tara's hand in sympathy. She knew slippery slopes all too well, "Oh my dear!"

Tara said, "I don't know what my future holds and I don't know how my marriage will pan out, but I am trying to give it a second chance. It is hard. It is no longer natural, it is a herculean effort for me, especially so now. But I am trying. *I miss Nutty in my heart. I miss him so much, it hurts me to the core every single day! But I have chosen this life that came with this man and I will make a go for it.*"

Tara looked at Ranvir across the room; their eyes met in acknowledgement. A strange quiet descended on her. In her fantasies, she would just walk away from her marriage and start a new life with Nutty. But in reality, it was easier said than done—she couldn't leave Neil behind. It also pained her to imagine letting Ranvir down because it would be a blow to him, especially now, when he too was making just as much an effort as she was to work things out.

She lit another cigarette, "Looking back, I realise that perhaps I had bought into the fantasy that happiness was something that I could acquire from an external source, that one man could be responsible for all my happiness. Maybe, it is many!"

"Amen to that! But *hey, take it easy,* okay?" Niharika quipped. "Tara, I am worried for you. But if you don't want your delicious husband, I will be happy to take him off your hands!"

"Ha ha!... Very funny!"

As if on cue, the waiter came by with a tray of champagne flutes. "Champagne, ladies?"

They grabbed a glass each. "Cheers! To us! To *Cupidity*!" Niharika smiled.

Tara raised her glass, "To the Cupidians!"

Having made her resolve to stick on her path of fixing her marriage at all costs, she felt at peace with herself. She walked across to Ranvir and hugged him, "Ranvir! Happy Birthday darling! Cheers to the both of us! I can't tell you how happy I am to have you back in Delhi."

Ranvir took her in his arms and kissed her on the nape of her neck and whispered in her ear, "Tara, it feels so nice to be home with you. I can't even tell you how much I've missed you. I truly love... Let's make this thing right between us."

The party ended in the wee hours. Tara was helping the houseboy clean up for the night. She was tired and wanted to take a shower and get into bed.

Ranvir was already in bed and he called out to her, "Tara, you must be tired. Why don't you leave the rest for tomorrow and come to bed. It's Sunday tomorrow, after all. Do all your cleaning then."

"Coming…give me a minute. I'm nearly done with this." Tara entered the room. She was in a more decisive state of mind, *this is it—my marriage comes first and I'm seriously going to make an effort*. She was hot, tired and went in for a shower to freshen up and 'get into the mood'. She decided to put on her black lingerie and light a few candles in the room.

Just as she walked into the dressing area, her mobile beeped. She looked down; it was a message from Nutty, "I miss you. Let's meet next Saturday. I want you. Let's try and make this work between us. Let's talk."

Tara stood there for a long time. *What are the chances? Is this serendipity? I spoke of you today after a long time…and here you are*. All her earlier resolve vanished into thin air. She had tried for a very long time not to meet Nutty but he had her in a vice; she was emotionally and mentally hooked onto him. It was a spontaneous thing with Nutty. Nothing was planned or calculated. Neither of them had ever been unfaithful before and so it seemed like such a big step, but inevitably it had to happen.

It dawned upon her that Ranvir and she were just not on the same page. Maybe Ranvir came home few years too late. Now that she had him where she wanted him for so long, the present day Tara didn't want him here anymore. There was too much water under the bridge, she had moved on. Her heart was heavy… Tears dropped down for all that she had lost. *Is this what 17 years of marriage with Ranvir had come to?*

She read and re-read the message from Nutty over and over again. She felt a rush of adrenalin flow through her, like fire. She felt alive and vibrant and loved how every pore of her being responded to him.

She looked at herself in the mirror and thought, *What the heck! Life is short to make excuses. I am going to do what makes me happy. I'm getting on in age and I want companionship with someone who I can connect with, talk to, share my life with. I feel beautiful, special, and so wanted and understood by him.*

She messaged him back, "Yes! Miss you too. Can't wait for next Saturday!"

After sending the message, she told herself, *No one else need ever know. This would be my very own secret.*

A private space, deep in the recesses of her mind, where she could be herself, explore her sexuality, her dreams and her desires. What she got out of him was fun, passion and a confirmation that she was worth more than a cook, cleaner, an agony aunt, a wife and a mother. She was constantly thinking about him from the moment she woke up to the moment she finally feel asleep.

She heard Ranvir call her, "Tara, what's taking you so long?"

Keeping a straight face and with a duplicity that even she didn't know she possessed, she replied back. Her tone sounded steady, "Coming Ranvir. Why don't you go to sleep? I'll be there in a few minutes."

She then went into her message history and deleted all of Nutty's messages from the message log. She looked at herself in the mirror and couldn't recognise the person staring back at her. She asked herself, *Is this the point when I should start feeling guilty?* Strangely, she didn't feel anything except a deep sense of purpose. She smiled surreptitiously and said to herself, *You adulteress…you wicked woman!…The game begins now and it's well worth it.*

Acknowledgements

It has been a long, well worded, journey for the both of us. In spite of the initial hiccups, we made it, in total awe of each other's creative processes and for the benefit of creative collaboration.

We thank our online suitors, unwitting targets, who haplessly strung along without knowing that they were being used as *masala* for the book. Some of them have become good friends, the others, we would like to acknowledge.

Madhvi acknowledges all the naughty smiles with air quotes, "RESEARCH?" Kiren gives surety to her worried lot, "*My marriage is in good stead and I'm not planning to run away into the virtual.*"

We thank our family and friends who took us through this jungle of words. You know who you are, bless you for being such patient sounding boards. We can't wait for you to see the final product.

We doff our hats to two creative geniuses, we admire, Ginni Xanders, for all book-related design, and Manav Parhawk, for our fantastic photographs.

We also thank the lovely staff of Le Bistro Du Parc, New Delhi, for being the perfect hosts to us, budding authors, who sat for hours and wrote in peace.

We thank Ajay Mago, our publisher, from Om Books International, and the editor-in-chief, Dipa Chaudhuri, for their constant encouragement and valuable inputs.

A big 'Thank you' to all of you.